"I've missed he said aga

Her head was swimming, and she was trembling against him. She wanted him and wished she didn't. She still wasn't sure what he thought of her, where she stood with him.

As his hands slipped beneath the flimsy material of her blouse, she moved away from his embrace. "I...think that's enough."

Adam's smile was a mixture of skepticism and genuine amusement. "Do you, Kate?" His brown eyes were glittering, looking straight into her. "It isn't nearly enough. You want me, but don't worry. I shan't let it go to my head. And I want you," he went on. "But you mustn't let it go to your head, either."

Kate stiffened, puzzled by his words and by his behavior. What had his last few words meant, exactly?

CLAUDIA JAMESON lives in Berkshire, England, with her husband and family. She is an extremely popular author in both the Harlequin Presents and Harlequin Romance series. And no wonder! Her lively dialogue and ingenious plots—with the occasional dash of suspense—make her a favorite with romance readers everywhere.

Books by Claudia Jameson

These books may be available at your local bookseller.

Don't miss any of our special offers. Write to us at the following address for information on our newest releases.

Harlequin Reader Service
901 Fuhrmann Blvd., P.O. Box 1397, Buffalo, NY 14240
Canadian address: P.O. Box 603,
Fort Erie, Ont. L2A 5X3

CLAUDIA JAMESON

adam's law

Harlequin Books

TORONTO • NEW YORK • LONDON
AMSTERDAM • PARIS • SYDNEY • HAMBURG
STOCKHOLM • ATHENS • TOKYO • MILAN

Harlequin Presents first edition January 1987
ISBN 0-373-10945-8

Original hardcover edition published in 1986
by Mills & Boon Limited

CHAPTER ONE

GUERNSEY airport was small but it was brightly lit and busier than she had expected. Kate Sumner hated crowds. Worse, she was looked at by every one of the people lined up to meet the passengers from her flight.

Aunt Dolly was not among them.

Flinching from the second looks she was getting, Kate hauled her large suitcases into a corner and stood by them. She was half facing the wall, positioned so she could keep her back to the other people while keeping an eye open for her aunt. Where *was* she? Why wasn't she here? How could she be so thoughtless as to leave Kate waiting in public? She could almost hear people's comments about her, 'Nice figure, shame about the face . . .'

There was little Kate could do about either. Even in a bulky, full-length coat she couldn't hide her figure. It was a hideous coat, too, she had bought it specially for this journey and it was brown, the one colour which had never suited her. She no longer dressed to attract, to raise eyebrows, she no longer wanted to stand out in a crowd. A tall, willowy girl, her deportment was the result of training but her gracefulness was innate. Disguising any of this was difficult; it would take time, practice, to learn how to hide what was left of her attractiveness.

The only thing that shielded her face from onlookers was the sheet of silky, blue-black hair. It just touched her shoulders now, and was parted on the right, so that the bulk of it fell across her left cheek. It didn't cover the patchwork of tiny scars, not all of them, but it helped partially to obscure the yellow-brown bruise which spread right around her eye to her temple.

5

She'd had twelve inches cut off her hair since the accident. Not so long ago it had been almost waist-length, one of her most attractive features, a long mane with which she'd been able to create many different styles. She laughed hollowly at the thought. One of her most attractive features? Some had said so. Others had said it was her eyes, so blue they were almost violet. They were fringed with lashes as black as soot, long lashes which became unbelievably long when touched with mascara. There again, some people had thought her mouth her prettiest feature, whilst others thought her beauty lay in her bone structure. So much attention! As a photographic model she had had so much attention, admiration, *success*! Her face had appeared on the covers and in the pages of countless magazines. And now, now it was ruined . . .

Where are you, Dolores? Aunt Dolly, where *are* you?

Kate glanced at her watch. Her aunt was in fact only five minutes late—so far. What was five minutes? It was an eternity to Kate. It was agonising, standing there in the main concourse of an airport, albeit a tiny one compared to some she had been in.

'You're not Miss Crowther, are you?' a young man asked. 'For the St Margaret's Lodge Hotel?'

'No. I—no.' Kate turned her attention back to her watch, a blush suffusing her face. She had seen it again, the look of surprise followed by pity in the eyes of a stranger. She would never get used to it, *never*. She had been out of the private nursing home in London for only two days but—but she had yet to encounter someone, anyone, who did not gaze at her with pity. Even those who looked at her with open curiosity, like the stewardess on the flight she'd just been on, ended up averting their eyes. And the question was always there, unspoken, 'What happened? What happened to you?' Even her parents had looked at her with incredible sadness. They, who had known what to expect when they'd visited her in the nursing home. And what they'd seen had been a vast improvement compared to the way she'd looked when she'd been in hospital in Bristol.

'Oh, thank God!' On spotting Aunt Dolly, she picked up her cases and walked quickly towards her, wanting only to get out of this public place.

Dolores de la Mare was in fact her great aunt, her mother's aunt. She was tiny, rotund, possessed of great energy and mild eccentricity. She was sixty-one years old but there wasn't a grey hair in her head. Born in Leeds, where Kate's mother originated, Aunt Dolly was the youngest of three sisters and had been a spinster until the age of thirty-six. Having looked after her ailing mother until then, and full-time at that, she had fulfilled a dream after her mother's death and had gone on holiday to Kenya. There, so the story went, she had gone on safari and afterwards had met in Nairobi her future husband, a widower, a Guernseyman who was on holiday with his son. All that had been years ago, before Kate was born.

Dolores and Roland de la Mere had had no children of their own and Kate had never met her aunt's stepson, Adam, who lived in Tuscany in Italy these days. She knew quite a lot about him, though, he was Dolly's pride and joy, someone she talked about far too much—understandable though it was. Not everyone had a famous sculptor for a stepson.

Kate had met her great uncle Roland only twice, on the two occasions he and Dolly had come to stay with her parents in Bristol. He rarely left Guernsey. He had died three years earlier and he was someone else Dolly talked about often, with pride and never with tears. 'We had twenty-two years together,' she had said to Kate in the hospital in December. 'And, given my late start and Roland's seniority, I couldn't have expected much more. I loved every single day of it. And I have Adam. He rings me regularly from Italy, you know.'

'I'm sorry, dear,' her aunt said now. 'My meeting went on longer than it should have and then I had to go home to feed the animals, which was fine except that a neighbour popped in for a chat and—oh, dear! Am I dreadfully late? Did you have a nice flight? The car's outside. I'm parked illegally but it's so difficult here— what did you say? Give me those suitcases.'

Kate was perspiring, not that it was hot. It was February and it had been freezing in London. The short walk from the plane to the airport building had told her that the climate was a little milder here in the Channel Islands. Her parents had said it would be. In years past they had spent the odd week here but Kate had never been to the island before. She had always had something better to do, she supposed, holidays with the school or staying with her friends or something. The idea of staying with an old uncle and aunt and a boy years older than herself had not exactly appealed when she was a youngster. In fact, until quite recently Dolly had been hardly more than a name to her. It was only at her brother Thomas's wedding last year that she had got to know her aunt a little.

The hefty coat, her anxiety and general weakness of body were combining to make her perspire, to feel light-headed. And her neck was still stiff, her leg was throbbing—but she was smiling. She was smiling more than she had in weeks, knowing great relief at her aunt's appearance and profound gratitude for her casual chatter.

They climbed into a rather battered Volvo estate. Kate's suitcases were shoved into the back—with two labradors—and they drove off in a cacophony of barking, music from the car radio and Aunt Dolly's questions as to Kate's health.

Thank heavens, thank heavens for her, Kate thought. Thank heavens for some normality, for this blessed escape from London, from Bristol, from memories, terror and, please God, from the recurring nightmare. And from her so-called friends. All she wanted to do was to hide on this tiny island where nobody knew her. To hide and, hopefully, to heal. As much as she was going to heal. There was the possibility of another operation ahead of her, plastic surgery, but she'd been told not to hope for too much.

She was weak with relief, now she was ensconced safely in her aunt's car. Never again would she enjoy riding in a car, but at least she hadn't developed a phobia about it.

'I'm all right, really.' She spoke above the music. 'I'm just tired, that's all.' Tired, she certainly was. Disinclined to talk, too. Besides, she didn't want to list her aches and pains to her aunt. Not to mention her fears. How could she say, at twenty-one, that her life was over? People would scorn her, even her lovely, understanding aunt. But that's what it felt like. What was there, now? The accident had smashed not only her face, her career, her confidence, it had also destroyed her future, a glowing future . . .

Happily Aunt Dolores talked enough for them both. 'You're very pale but your face is looking better.' She stated this with a nod, taking her eyes from the road to look straight at Kate.

It was twilight. Wait till she saw it in the broad light of day. 'I—let's not talk about it.' Kate turned away. It was difficult to allow even Dolly's scrutiny. Dolly, who looked at her with love, not pity.

She had such a big heart, such a generous nature. When she'd turned up at the hospital in Bristol, only days after the accident, Kate had been at a loss to understand the woman's motives. The two of them were not close, they didn't know one another well enough for that, so why had she come all that way?

'To give moral support,' had been the answer. 'To your mother as well as to you. She phoned and told

me what happened. She's beside herself with anxiety. I
know all about your hysterics, Kate. I know you'll need
to recuperate from your injuries—the emotional ones
especially. I'm here to tell you you can come to me.
Stay with me in Guernsey, if you like. You can live with
me until you get yourself together. You can stay as long
as you wish and you'll be looked after, have a good rest
and lots of peace. At least, you'll have peace when I'm
out of the house, which is often!'

Beyond a feeling of gratitude, Kate hadn't responded
at the time. There had been too much to think about,
too much haunting her. There still was. She had
thanked her aunt but had not committed herself.
Dolores hadn't wanted her to do either. Her offer was,
simply, there.

And now Kate was here. To hide.

'We'll be home in five minutes. It's only ten minutes
from the airport to the house. We're in St Peter's now.
There's the parish church. See the stained glass
windows? It's beautiful, isn't it?'

Kate grunted. She wasn't exactly into churches. She
saw a sign: *St Pierre du Bois*. Translated into English,
St Peter in the Wood. The locals called it St Peter's,
apparently. Feeling obliged to show a little interest, she
asked, 'How come all the road names are in French?
And the house names? I haven't seen one in English
yet.' The houses looked pretty, actually. There were a
lot of granite ones around, others were painted in white
and pastel colours. So this was Guernsey? An odd little
island. There were palm trees here but their fronds were
blowing in the strong, cold wind. Maybe the summers
were hot. It was and it was not like England. If you
took away all the French and the palm trees, it could
resemble an English village, she supposed, but there
again ... 'I thought the official language was English
here?'

'Only since 1921. It had been—oops!'

Kate blinked in surprise. Ahead of them was a herd of cows being led across the road by a ruddy-faced farmer. He waved at Dolly and touched his cap deferentially. She waved back vigorously. 'Mr Rihoy,' she informed Kate as he and his cows got out of the way. 'A lovely man. What was I saying? Oh, yes—about the language. English had been gradually taking over prior to that, of course. You won't hear much Guernesiais these days. The old people still——'

'Guernesiais?'

'Guernsey-French. It's not like modern French, it's nearer to that spoken by the Normans in the eleventh and twelfth centuries! Not easy to understand. Seventy-five years ago that's all you'd have heard out here in the country parishes, but not now. Sad, isn't it? The war's to blame mostly. So many children were evacuated during the years when the islands were occupied, the language didn't get passed on to them. Well, there are differing opinions as to whether it's a language or a patois. Roland spoke it, of course, and Adam has a smattering of it. He's the one to talk to about Guernsey, you know. He's——'

She never finished the sentence. She pulled the car to one side, tucking it neatly into a passing place so an oncoming vehicle could get by. Vehicle? It was a tractor. And its driver waved to Dolly and Dolly waved back.

The roads were unbelievable now! Since leaving the main road from the airport, they had got narrower and narrower and the one they'd just turned on to was wide enough for only one car. The next one was even narrower. It seemed to Kate that the parish of St Peter in the Wood was a network of intricately laced country lanes which all looked alike. She couldn't see any woods, as such. Beyond the lanes were fields, greenhouses. In fact, there seemed to be greenhouses everywhere.

'Did your mum tell you what to expect?' her aunt was asking.

'She didn't mention all these greenhouses!' Kate smiled. 'She did tell me the speed limit is thirty-five miles an hour here. I can see why.'

Dolly laughed at that. 'It's twenty-five in built-up areas. But that isn't what I meant. I was talking about the house. Do you know I've had the kitchen and bathrooms modernised? Last year. It cost the earth but Adam insisted. He said it was time I made life easier for myself, more comfortable. He has some odd ideas!'

Kate looked curiously at her aunt. 'Why is that an odd idea?'

'Because I was perfectly comfortable to begin with. Roland didn't like change, you know. Not that Adam does, but of course he is a man of today. A modern man. Ah, but he's still a Guernseyman at heart, very much so!' And with that, she rolled her eyes heavenward.

Kate turned her attention to the scenery. Aunt Dolly was a bit eccentric, her mother had always said so. She was making no sense at all just now, but no doubt she knew what she was talking about. Eccentric, she might be. Stupid, she was not. She was assuming that Kate knew what 'a Guernseyman' meant. Kate didn't bother to try and decipher what had just been said. She wasn't sufficiently interested.

Her aunt's next words were more than interesting, however. They were, to Kate, appalling. 'I'm sorry Adam won't be in when we get home. He's out flying at the moment.'

'Flying? What——' She got no further. Her heart sank into her boots. Adam de la Mare was in Italy, wasn't he?

He was not. 'Mm. You know Adam—oh, no, you don't, do you?' A little laugh, an indulgent one. 'Well, if he isn't working, he's flying, if he isn't flying, he's working. And if that's the way he chooses to run his life, who am I to criticise?'

'But—but I had no idea he was here. I mean—I thought he lived in Italy?' Kate finished the sentence lamely. Who was *she* to protest? Oh, but she was disappointed! She had believed there would be solitude here, just her and an aunt who spent a lot of time at meetings, charity things, doing meals-on-wheels and whatever. In other words, she thought she'd be alone most of the time.

'He does, but only for six months of the year. I thought you knew that? He came home a few days ago. Adam likes to spend spring and summer on his native soil, he always comes home from March to September.'

It was only February. Kate could hardly point that out without sounding sullen, resentful. But she was. She felt almost as if she'd been tricked into coming here— which was, of course, ridiculous. An ungrateful thought. Instead she said, 'Well, I—I look forward to meeting him at long last.'

Dolores was oblivious to her niece's lie. She was so enamoured of her stepson, she probably couldn't imagine anyone not wishing to meet him. Kate had nothing against the man, she just wished he were in Italy.

'Adam is a very private person.' Aunt Dolly was frowning. 'And as I say, he's a Guernseyman, so I don't——'

'Aunt Dolly, I don't know what that means.'

'For one thing it means he's stubborn, for another it means he doesn't take easily to outsiders.'

Kate was glad to hear it. Family or no, she hoped Adam would regard her as an outsider. She had no desire to be 'taken to' by him. She absolutely did not want to be in the company of a stranger, most especially one of the opposite sex.

'So I don't want you to think he's brusque. I mean,

he can appear that way at times. Ignore it, Kate, if
that's the impression you get. It's just his way. Basically
he's loving and generous and kind. He'd do anything
for me, you know, anything in the world! He's such . . .'

Kate groaned inwardly. She had switched off, lost
interest in her surroundings and what her aunt was
telling her now. It went in one ear and out the other,
the glowing account she was giving of her stepson, the
sculptor, the highly talented, the brusque but loving and
generous, *et cetera, et cetera*.

As they turned into the driveway of the house, her
spirits lifted a little. It was old, a farmhouse built of
blue Guernsey granite, and it was big. It was big
enough to get lost in. It was flanked on either side by
giant conifers and the vast, sloping lawn in front was
dotted with trees and bushes, very much a casual,
country-garden. It was far removed from her parents'
neat patches of garden in Bristol and very far removed
from Kate's window boxes at her London flat!
Fleetingly, she saw another difference; in the centre of
the lawn was a life-sized statue on a pedestal, a long-
haired nude. One of A. E. de la Mare's? She couldn't be
sure, she had only seen his work in magazines and in
some photographs her mother had shown to her. She
couldn't be sure that the statue was in his style.

They drove around the house, to the back. There the
drive was wider and on it there was another vehicle, a
dirty, yellow pick-up truck. Aunt Dolly, whose husband
had been a land owner and one-time grower, was well
off according to Kate's mother. If that were the case, it
certainly didn't show in her choice of transport any
more than it showed in her clothes. She had turned up
at the airport in a pair of gum-boots and an ancient
sheepskin coat covered with hairs.

Kate's eyes moved around quickly, taking in the
gardens and fields to the side and the back of the
house, the greenhouse, the speedboat which was resting

on a metal contraption with wheels, the woodstack, sheds and a building which looked like stables down at the bottom of the field. In the near distance, beyond the field, was a hill on which she could just make out the two white goats tethered there. In the field which went with the house, two more goats were tethered. These two were her aunt's, she was told.

As she got out of the car, she again had qualms about having come here, for different reasons now. It was so—so *quiet*! It was like a different world. The early winter darkness was descending and it seemed as if nothing were moving anywhere. She couldn't even hear the sound of another car, in any direction. It was very, very different from the hustle and bustle she'd been used to, the busy, glamorous life she'd led. Could she stand it? She was a city girl through and through, would she be bored out of her mind here?

The idea was quickly pushed aside. If she weren't here, what else would she be doing? What else could she do? What could she do with her time, her life, now? She had nothing to fall back on, no talent for anything except modelling. Her days of glamour, of wine and roses, were over.

'Adam is home, after all. That's his truck.' Aunt Dolly was stabbing a finger in the direction of the pickup while opening the back of her car at the same time. The dogs bounded out, tails wagging because they were free at last. They proceeded to give Kate the welcome—and inspection—they'd been unable to give her in the car, thanks to the wire mesh which separated them from the passenger and driver. She patted them a little tentatively. Never having had a dog of her own, she wasn't really sure whether she liked them, though these two labradors were very handsome to look at.

'What—what are they called, Aunt Dolores?'

'Buster and Bruce.'

Kate almost jumped out of her skin. The voice came

from immediately behind her and it wasn't that of her
aunt. She spun round like a frightened rabbit, her hair
flying right across her face. In one movement she
straightened, her hand reaching for the errant hair,
holding it in place against the wind. She found herself
looking up, a long way up, into brown eyes in a craggy
but good-looking face. 'I—you startled me. I suppose
you're Adam?'

She hadn't paused to think, to put the question a
little more graciously.

He did not offer his hand. He simply stood, hands
shoved deep into the pockets of washed out denims.
Nodding curtly, he said, 'And I suppose you're Kate?'

She tried to make amends. Her face was going red
again and panic was setting in. His scrutiny of her was
intense, it revealed no emotion at all but it disconcerted
her just the same. She knew what he was thinking, she
always knew what people thought when they looked at
her these days. Still holding her hair in place with one
hand, she shifted her eyes to the region of his feet and
held out her right hand. 'Yes. Kate Sumner.'

'Adam de la Mare.' He took her hand briefly but
there was time for her to feel the roughness of his skin.
Then he moved away from her.

Aunt Dolly was laughing at them. 'How very formal
you are!'

'I'll take those, Mum.' Adam reached for the
suitcases.

Kate's eyebrows shot up in surprise. She hadn't
expected him to call Dolly 'Mum'. Not that she'd
actually thought about it, it just—seemed odd. Yet why
should it? Dolores had been a mother to him since he
was—what? Around ten or eleven, she supposed.

He had to be in his middle thirties now. A giant of a
man, Kate watched him while appearing to resume her
fuss over the dogs. At five feet nine, she didn't meet
many men to whom she had to look up such a long

way. Adam had to be six-four if he were an inch. She hadn't realised this, even though she had seen photographs of him. He was better looking than his photos, and blonder. Blond mingled with grey, by the look of it. Last year, only two weeks before she herself had appeared in *The Times* colour supplement, in a close up photograph advertising make-up, there had been an article about A. E. de la Mare: 'Adam Eugene de la Mare—An Artist at Work'. He had been photographed and interviewed at his home in Tuscany, a villa set in beautiful countryside.

In the flesh, he was nothing like she'd imagined him to be. He didn't look like a sculptor to her, he looked like a lumberjack with that massive chest and broad back. There was nothing at all about him which denoted the sensitivity of an artist. Even his voice was like gravel.

'If you'll follow me, Kate, I'll show you to your room. I'm sure the first thing Dolly will do is put the kettle on. It has boiled,' he added, speaking over his shoulder to his stepmother.

They trooped into the house through a side door which led straight into the kitchen, a vast kitchen which ran the depth of the house. Its main windows overlooked the front garden.

'How come you're home already?' Dolly was asking. 'I thought you'd gone flying?'

Adam paused to answer her and Kate almost collided with him. 'I didn't say that, I said I was going to the aero club. It's too windy to fly today, Mum, you should have realised that.'

'So I should,' came the cheerful reply. 'Silly me! I've been up often enough, haven't I?'

'Don't make any tea for me. I'm going out. Won't be back for dinner, either.'

'All right, dear.'

There followed one more word—Kate's name. She

didn't imagine the brusqueness in the single syllable, it was spoken as if he were calling one of the dogs to heel. She trooped after him, smoothing her wind-blown hair as she walked.

He stopped by a door in the middle of the long, first-floor landing. It ran the width of the house and opened on to half a dozen rooms or more. 'Your room.'

She nodded, opening the door because his hands were occupied with her suitcases.

'Just a minute.' Putting the cases down, he jerked his head in the direction of the next door. Kate caught another glimpse of brown eyes before looking away.

Adam showed her the next door bathroom. 'You have this to yourself. Dolly has a bathroom en suite and my rooms,' he paused, jerking his head again, this time in the direction of the gable end of the house, 'are there.'

Kate caught the message in his tone: so don't come blundering in. He had said nothing to make her feel welcome, only like an intruder.

She didn't care, but it got worse. He led the way into her bedroom and plonked her two cases on the bed as if they were full of fresh air. Then he walked over to the windows and flung them open. A cold blast of wind came at her. 'I suppose this room's all right for you? There is a sea view—just.'

Kate stayed where she was. She wasn't interested in a sea-view and she was unmoved by his coldness. He was making sure she felt like an intruder. Well, this was Dolly's house and she was Dolly's guest. To hell with him. She wouldn't get under his feet, if that was what worried him. 'It's fine, thank you.'

Nothing else was said. Adam de la Mare was clearly a man of few words. That was fine by her. He wouldn't ruffle her, she simply wasn't interested enough in—in anything—to get upset. After what she'd been through, sharing a roof with a dour Guernseyman would be an absolute doddle.

CHAPTER TWO

ALONE, she marched over to the windows and shut them. Yes, she could see the sea, over the tops of the trees which separated one field from another, down to the left at the back of the house. In fact, if she looked to the left of the hill she could see for miles over the English Channel.

Turning away, she tried to be enthusiastic about her room. The floor was wooden and covered with colourful rugs. There was a fire burning in the grate. The bed was a four-poster, a really old one. She sat on it, bounced on it. The mattress wasn't old, it was very comfortable.

On the white-washed, roughly plastered walls there were paintings and photographs of the island's bays and coves. Kate inspected them one by one before drawing the curtains. Heavens, it was so quiet here . . . How on earth had Dolores adjusted to life here, a city girl who had spent her first thirty-six years in Leeds?

The room was cosy. The real fire, the paintings, the chintzy curtains and bedspread, the soft glow of the lamps all combined to make a comfortable and cosy atmosphere. She *would* be all right here.

Dolly's voice came floating up the stairs. 'Kate? You're not unpacking, are you? I thought I'd help you with that later. Tea's up!'

'Coming.' She shed her coat, pulled a brush from her bag and dragged it through her hair. More than anything, all she wanted to do right now was to sleep. The flight from Heathrow had taken only fifty-five minutes and yet she was shattered. She hadn't regained her strength yet, not fully.

Her eyes moved to the mirror in the oak dressing table. Reluctantly, she went to sit before it in order to get her parting straight. Looking in mirrors was something she avoided doing these days. She was no masochist, there was no way she could adjust to her new looks, to the hideous flaws.

Her beauty had earned her a lot of money but it had never, ever, gone to her head. But, when one has always been pointed at as being exceptionally attractive, how does one not take it for granted? She'd been pretty as a child, lovely as a teenager and ... and it seemed so unfair that now, at twenty-one, when her best years should be ahead of her ... No, not unfair. Deserved. If she'd had her seat belt fastened, as the law required, her face would have been spared. She had been told as much.

She'd been drunk that night, the night of her twenty-first birthday, carefree, happy, but Roger hadn't been drunk. Roger Dennison had been doing the driving. Roger, who was a superb driver and who had been honestly, totally, sober. He was a teetotaller.

The trouble was that Kate's birthday was the twentieth of December and the Christmas period, the days before it and after New Year are probably the most treacherous ones as far as driving is concerned. Other drivers drink. There was ice on the roads. Kate and her boyfriend had been in Bristol for the party her parents were giving for her twenty-first. If only she and Roger had stayed in Bristol, if only they hadn't decided to go back to London the same night. If only she hadn't had too much to drink, she'd never have insisted on getting to London, to another party which they knew would be going on all night long.

If onlys were no good. If onlys were too late. What was done was done. A car crash was a car crash and she'd been lucky to come out of it alive. Lucky? One broken leg, six cracked ribs, two broken fingers ... and a shattered cheekbone. On the left. Countless stitches in the area. A very near miss from unthinkable damage to her eye.

Three weeks in a Bristol hospital. Several weeks in a private London nursing home. Enormous medical bills for which she had not yet had any compensation, insurance. Her father, a solicitor, was handling that business for her. One operation and the promise, or threat, of another. Possible improvement. 'I'll refer you to a plastic surgeon,' the doctor in Bristol had said, 'in Harley Street. Go and see him in three months or so, he'll decide what's to be done. Much will depend on how the scar tissue heals in the meantime . . .'

No matter what improvement they made to the angry red scars, her career as a photographic model was over. Any kind of modelling was out of the question. Her figure might be fantastic, but who wanted a scar-faced model, even for a clothes-horse? No more appearances in Sunday magazines, no more advertisements on television, no more high-life, no more——

'Kate? All you all right, dear?'

'Yes, I—I'm sorry, I'm just coming.'

She hurried downstairs.

Two days passed before she saw Adam again. What she hadn't realised was that he worked here in Guernsey as well as in Tuscany. What used to be a stable block in her aunt's grounds was now a studio and had been for some years.

Kate never went near it. Adam rarely surfaced from it. The weather continued to be windy, and wet, and so his flying had to wait for a while. He had, she learned from Dolores, a four-seater, single-engined Cessna, a light aircraft which didn't take kindly to too much buffeting from the wind. The idea of flying in such a machine would once have excited Kate, but not now.

Now, the very thought of it gave her the shudders. Only one engine? And what if it failed?

Dolores, however, loved going for a 'spin', as she put it. As her aunt's character opened up before her, Kate was continually astonished. Dolores was up with the crack of dawn, feeding her goats, digging in her greenhouse, planting, uprooting, preparing vegetables, walking the dogs, going off to meetings, raising money for charities—the list was endless. One thing she was not enthusiastic about was housework.

It wasn't that the house was dirty, far from it, it was just—somewhat chaotic, especially in the living-room. Unlike the kitchen and bathrooms, the living-room was not modern, it was a big room with vast windows overlooking the back gardens and fields and its furniture was old-fashioned but good quality, well cared for and very comfy. And yet there was some kind of order in the chaos in here. At least, there was to her aunt. Kate supposed it was just a question of memory—remembering where everything was! Apart from the plants and myriad photographs, ornaments and small sculptures, there were stacks of magazines, photograph albums and what seemed like a million books in the living-room, and Aunt Dolly could put her hand on anything she wanted, instantly. She produced several books and magazine articles which she thought would interest her niece—and so Kate found herself reading all day. And she was happy to do so. Aunt Dolly's library ranged from the classics through to modern blockbusters and Kate had the opportunity of doing something she'd always intended to do, one day. To catch up on all the books she'd wished she'd read. She started with the works of Jane Austen, (Aunt Dolly had them all). She found that she wasn't bored, much to her relief. She was glad to have time on her hands for once.

Adam de la Mare tried to spoil that pleasure. He

came into the living-room during the mid-morning of Kate's third day. 'Oh, it's you. Where's Dolly?'

Kate glanced at him over the top of *Mansfield Park*, the hardback she was reading. She wanted to say, 'And a good morning to you, too,' but she didn't. It wasn't worth the aggro and she wanted to keep the peace. 'Out. She's gone into St Peter Port. Didn't you hear her drive off?'

'Town,' he amended. 'If you don't wish to be classed as a tourist, you never say "St Peter Port".'

'What's wrong with being a tourist?' She didn't look at him. She had seen enough. Today he looked like a farmer except for the bits of plaster and clay which stained the smock he was wearing.

'Nothing. They're good for the island's economy. Did she say when she'll be back?'

'No. For lunch, I expect.'

'Don't *expect* anything with Dolly. If you have it in mind to eat, you help yourself in this house, unless definite arrangements are made. We come and go as we please and we do our own thing, okay?'

Kate had already gathered that. She'd had dinner with Dolly each evening but Adam had stayed in his studio so far. When she'd seen her aunt going down there with a cooked meal on a tray, she'd worried. She'd asked her aunt whether that were usual. 'Oh, yes,' came the reply. 'Sometimes he doesn't eat at all, sometimes he eats down there, sometimes in here with me. He might work all night or he might lay off for a couple of days. I don't question his methods.'

That was the sweetest thing about her aunt. She was extremely easy-going and she let Kate do exactly as she pleased.

Adam was still in the doorway of the living-room. When next he spoke, his irritation was very obvious. 'Do you think, for once, you could look at me when you speak to me?'

Kate raised her head a little. 'I—thought our conversation was over.'

'Which is not the point,' he snapped, walking away.

A few days later he said something similar. Again Kate was in the armchair, reading. This time it was *Sense and Sensibility* she was into when Adam disturbed her.

'So you've finally got out of bed?'

'I'm here to rest.' Kate answered, not bothering to look up.

'Is that any reason why you should sit aroudn in an old housecoat all day?'

'I can't see how that affects you,' she said, polite but cool.

'What's the matter with you? I don't trust people who constantly avoid my eyes, Kate. I tend to think they're sly, shifty. Dishonest.'

'That's your hang-up.' She was into her book again. His next remark brought her head up swiftly, however, so that she was not only looking at him, she was staring at him.

'Don't you think,' he drawled, leaning against the door-jamb and peering at her, 'that it's high time you started getting over your hang-up? If you're so concerned about your looks, why don't you go the whole hog and put a sack over your head? You could cut two holes in it so you can keep on reading.'

He'd gone before she was breathing normally again. Her breath seemed to be stuck in her chest. For pity's sake, she couldn't have heard correctly, could she? How cruel! How bloody *cruel* could a person *be*?

He had cut her to the quick and tears sprang into her eyes. The next thing she knew, he was calling to her from the kitchen. Bellowing, more like. 'I'm making coffee, do you want some?'

Kate didn't answer, she couldn't believe anyone could be so unkind. But she wasn't going to let him know how much he'd hurt her. Pushing her aunt's black and white cat from her lap, she got up and left the room via the door which led into the hall—bypassing the kitchen.

Once inside the safety of her room she sat on an armchair, shaking. Depression swamped her, curling suddenly around her like a damp fog. How strange people were, how *strange*! How different everything was for her now. There had been a time when she'd been able to wrap any normal, red-blooded man around her finger. Never in her life had she been short of compliments, attention, admiration. And now—now there were insults, terrible disappointments from people. Not that anyone had hurt her as Adam just had.

But even Roger, who had got off astonishingly lightly from the accident, had let her down. She had been dating him, among others because she always played the field, for three months and he had declared his love for her on their third evening out. So much for that. He had visited her in the hospital in London, and she had refused to see him because she simply couldn't face him, couldn't face anyone other than family seeing her. And Roger hadn't come back. Oh, he'd sent her flowers regularly but he hadn't insisted on seeing her, he hadn't tried very hard . . .

Then, during the two nights she'd spent at her flat before leaving for Guernsey, he had turned up and suggested they didn't see each other for 'a while'. It was clear that his love for her had disappeared with her looks.

Her other so-called friends hadn't behaved much better. Again, they showered her with gifts and letters of sympathy but—they hadn't visited her. The top and bottom of it was that Kate was no longer one of the crowd. No longer a model in a modelling world of beautiful or talented people.

She didn't cry. She slept. Eventually. During her first couple of nights here she had lain awake for hours, thinking about the past and the future, bleak though it was. The silence had made sleep impossible, she was so unused to it, it seemed to scream at her in the dead of night.

The following evening found the three of them having dinner together. As was to be expected, Dolores kept the conversation going—almost single-handed.

'If you feel rested enough,' she said to Kate, 'perhaps you'd like to go out for a drive tomorrow. I'm longing to show you the island.'

Kate answered too quickly. 'No! That is, I—I don't really feel up to it. Not just yet.'

'As you wish, dear. I just hope you're not bored.'

Kate had her head down, aware of Adam's scrutiny. Unfortunately he was sitting opposite her and the light in the dining room was bright, it was one of those which hung low from the ceiling, right over the table. Sensing his irritation, which made no sense to her, she hurriedly explained herself to her aunt, about how it was nice she could catch up on years of neglected reading.

'I thought you were supposed to get some exercise— for your leg.' This came from Adam and it sounded like an accusation. Besides, what did he know of her physiotherapist's advice? She asked him.

'Have you always been so much on the defensive? Think about it. I know all the details of your accident.' He glanced at his stepmother, who had, of course, been given regular instalments of Kate's progress by her mother. 'What I'm saying is, you haven't once stepped outside this house since you got here. You've been here for days and you haven't put a foot outside the door. Literally.'

Experiencing another, rather long look from the

brown eyes in that craggy face, Kate looked away. Then she raised her eyes to his again and let them stay there. He wasn't going to rattle her, not again. He couldn't possibly hurt her any more than he already had. Pleasantly, she asked whether it were any of his business. 'Why should it affect you, how I spend my time?'

'It doesn't. But you bore me. I've never met anyone as boring, you haven't even got a decent conversation in you. Would you mind telling me why you've come to Guernsey?'

Dolores answered that. She looked puzzled. 'Kate's come to recuperate, dear. She's had a very bad time, you know.'

'I'm aware of that, too.' To Kate he said, 'But you're behaving as if it's the end of the world. There's a great deal of beauty around you, why don't you get off your backside and see some of it? Are you going to sit in an armchair for the next—however long you stay here? Like an invalid? You walk with a slight limp, in case you haven't noticed. Couldn't you push yourself to the end of the lane and back, for your own sake?'

Kate bit very hard into her cheeks. She put her soup spoon down. She wanted to cry, to run, to flee to her room again, but she was made of sterner stuff than that. Or was she? He could hurt her so easily and he seemed to take pleasure in doing so. What had happened to her? Had she undergone some kind of personality change during the past, awful, couple of months? Heavens, there had been a time when she'd have given this man *twice* as good as he gave her! But now ... now she didn't really know how to answer him. Her confidence had totally disintegrated. She couldn't even look at him now, even briefly.

'You—you told me that you, we, all do our own thing in this house. Will you bear that in mind, please?' She

picked up her spoon, hoping nobody would notice how
her hand was shaking.

It didn't seem possible but Dolores was oblivious to
the tension, oblivious to the way Kate was hurting.
Was her bias towards her stepson such that she would
allow him to insult people at her own table? Yes,
apparently.

And Adam de la Mare hadn't finished with her yet.
'And that's another thing that I find pathetic about
you, Kate.'

Kate carried on with her soup.

'Kate?'

She took a slow, deep breath. 'I'm not a mind reader.
Go on. You're going to tell me, so get on with it.'

'Your hair. The way you wear it like a curtain. I'm
finding it extremely offensive sitting opposite someone
who's got vegetable broth on her hair. Every time
your spoon goes to your mouth, your hair gets in the
way. You should see yourself. I'm expecting you any
minute to swallow a mouthful and have a coughing fit.
I don't know why you bother, it doesn't hide your
scars. You're kidding yourself if you think it's a
camouflage job.'

Stunned into a reaction, Kate got to her feet. She did so
with as much dignity as she could muster. To her aunt she
said, very quietly, 'Forgive me, I'll help myself from the
kitchen and take the rest of my dinner in my room.
I'm——' She was about to add that the last thing in the
world she wanted was to offend Adam. But sarcasm
would serve only to hurt Dolly. He, evidently, was
impervious to it. And she had no wish to hurt her aunt or
make her aware of an atmosphere. 'I'm tired,' she said
instead. 'And I'll sleep as soon as I've finished eating.'

It wasn't until the early hours that she slept, briefly,
and until then, she was anguished. For reasons best
known to himself, Adam didn't want her here. She
couldn't imagine why, she didn't get in his way, she had

never been anywhere near his studio, she did nothing to offend him. Well, it was hard luck. She wasn't going home. Facing solitude in London, the embarrassment of 'friends' who didn't want to see her, the crowd of which she was no longer a part, or hundreds of people who knew her in Bristol, was more than she could handle. Except for *his* presence, it was ideal for her here. *Why* had he taken such a dislike to her? She wasn't *that* bad to look at! Did she offend his artist's eye, perhaps? And what had he meant when he'd said she hadn't got a decent conversation in her? Chance would be a fine thing.

For just a few moments her feeling of anguish and hurt gave way to one of anger. What a supercilious swine he was! How dare he criticise her in such a lofty fashion? How dare he criticise her at *all*! 'Take a walk, for your own sake.' Imperious, arrogant devil! What the hell had it to do with him if she walked with a limp?

It was a sobering thought. Did she, in fact?

She put her untouched food to one side and stood. If she walked in a straight line in front of the full-length mirror in the wardrobe, she'd be able to tell. It certainly didn't feel as if she limped.

But why bother? She sat down again and picked up a book. So what if she didn't walk as well as she used to? It hardly mattered now.

Aunt Dolly didn't know the half of it, she was often out when her precious stepson made his cutting remarks to her niece. A couple of days later, when he came up to the house to fill his flask, he said, 'How long do you intend to stick around?'

Kate was writing a letter to her parents. 'As long as Aunt Dolly will have me.'

'I didn't mean that. I meant how long are you going to stay indoors? Why the hell don't you put some proper clothes on and get some fresh air? You look positively unhealthy—and you're too thin.'

'Thank you very much. But it's my problem, isn't it?'

'Indeed it is, Miss Sumner. And boy, have you got problems.'

Days came and went. February turned into March. They were just names on a calendar to Kate.

Her sleeping pattern continued to be erratic. Her nightmare recurred, twice. It was horrible, she would live again those few moments before the motorbike had hit the side of Roger's car. It had crunched into the passenger door as if making a bee-line for her. In reality she had seen it coming only for seconds, hurtling across a junction without stopping. In the dream she would see it over and over again, would feel the impact as the side of her face crashed against the window.

Sometimes she would sleep in the living-room during the day, exhausted, her hand on her open book. Other times she would go to bed early and sleep like the dead until the early hours. Then she would wake, at some ungodly time, and while away the wait until sun-up.

On the second occasion her nightmare came back, she woke up crying, perspiring, trembling. It was two in the morning and she went to stand by the open window. It was pitch black outside except for a half moon. There were no street lights around here, only the flashing of a lighthouse. She knew it was no good trying to sleep again, fear of the nightmare's return would keep her awake. Quietly she made her way to the kitchen and put some milk on to heat. She was just reaching for the brandy bottle in the kitchen cupboard when she heard the voice.

'Hitting the bottle now, are you?'

Gasping from shock, she almost dropped it. Adam had appeared from nowhere, without a sound. 'Where the devil did you come from?'

'I've been strolling round the grounds. You should try it some time.'

'You've been walking round in the pitch dark? At two in the morning? You must be mad.'

'There's plenty of moonlight. It's beautiful out there, but you wouldn't know about that, would you?' He leaned his huge frame against the fridge. 'What're you doing with the brandy at this time of night?'

Kate stepped to one side so he could see the pan on the stove. 'I'm not a secret drinker, if that's what you're thinking. It's to add to this milk—I haven't got used to the taste of goat's milk yet.'

He grunted at that. 'What woke you?'

'If you must know, I had a nightmare.'

'What kind of nightmare?'

She turned back to the stove and poured the milk. It was on the tip of her tongue to tell him to mind his own business for once, but she bit back the words. Never having lost her temper with him, she wasn't about to do so now. She handled him with her usual civility, albeit reluctantly. 'About the—my accident. I—it—comes back to haunt me from time to time.'

There was another grunt, a curt nod, a look of distaste on his face. 'It seems to me that goat's milk isn't the only thing you haven't got used to.'

'What does that mean?'

'It means,' he said, shoving himself into an upright position, 'that it's high time you started adjusting. You'll keep on being haunted, as you put it, until you learn to accept the changes in your life and face up to what happened. You can't hide away for ever, you know.'

He left. Kate stayed where she was, sipping at the milk and brandy. Oh, it was easy for him to talk! She just wished he would leave her alone and mind his own business. She hung around a moment longer, wanting to be sure he was out of the way before she went back to her room. It was a constant source of amazement to her that Adam de la Mare could be so obnoxious when

he had been brought up for so many years by someone
as nice as Dolores.

Aunt Dolly was lovely, as ever, cheerful, hard-
working and never in a mood. Adam continued not
only to be moody but also insulting. He chipped at her
just as he might at one of his much sought-after
sculptures, relentlessly, whenever their paths happened
to cross, which was usually when he came into the
house to fill his flask with coffee. Then, and on the
occasions he had a meal with them, when he wasn't
working or going out for the evening.

Kate withstood his attacks. From time to time anger
would make itself known to her again, but for the most
part it was buried beneath hopelessness. She reasoned
that for the little time she spent with the man, she might
as well let him have his fun. Sadist. He was obviously
sadistically inclined. Only once did she complain to her
aunt about his behaviour, his insults. They were often
subtle, so that Dolly didn't even look bemused, merely
unaware. But Kate caught each and every one of his
digs. Dig, dig. Chip, chip. It went on, and on, until one
day her aunt caught her weeping in the living-room.

'My darling Kate, whatever's the matter?'

'Him! It's *him*! I—why is he so horrid to me?'

'Horrid?' Kate was enfolded in a pair of chubby arms
and hugged almost breathless. 'There, now! I'm sure I
don't know what you mean. Adam's always been blunt,
always says what he's thinking. If he's hurt your feelings,
I'm sure he didn't mean to. He must think it's for the best.'

Kate stared at her aunt, incredulous. What was the
point? Adam simply couldn't do wrong in Dolly's eyes.

Her mother phoned every few days, asking how she
was, what she'd been doing. Kate wrote to her but the
fussing and phone calls continued. At least Dolly didn't
fuss, not like her mother. It sometimes seemed to Kate
that her accident and its result had been more
devastating for Anne Sumner than it had for herself.

Always, she placated her mother and gave a glowing report, saying she was well rested and feeling much better in herself. She was, after all, her parents' only daughter. Their worry was natural.

Still, in spite of her aunt's biased view of Adam, in spite of Adam himself, Kate was very glad indeed to be staying here on the island.

One morning, before six, she woke up and got up. It was dark outside, a little too early even for her aunt to be up and about, so she crept quietly downstairs and made a mug of coffee. She was creeping back when she came face to face with Adam.

They met in the hall. The grandfather clock which stood there was just chiming six. He was dressed in jeans and a navy-blue guernsey, a sweater made from oiled wool which is wind and shower resistant. She couldn't believe his greeting to her.

'Good morning, Kate. Bright and early, aren't you?'

At the way he smiled at her, she almost dropped her coffee. It was a total transformation. His teeth were beautiful, even and white, making his face seem browner than ever. He had that weather-beaten, rugged look. He looked like a fisherman today—except for the camera slung over his shoulder. Her eyes flicked over his straight, dark blond hair. It was too long at the back and it was far from neat, brushed straight from the forehead carelessly. But it suited him like that. He wasn't a neat sort of man. He was too—too big and bulky for that.

'I'm—yes, I am.' She made an effort, for her own sake as well as her aunt's. She had been understandably distant with him but she had always managed to be polite. Still, it would be so much nicer if she could start to get on with him. 'I'm hardly bright but I'm certainly early!' She smiled in return, she even managed not to touch her hair, not to turn her face to one side and avoid his eyes.

'I'm going flying at first light. The forecast's really good. Clear blue skies, do you fancy coming with me? I'm only doing a few circuits round the islands. You can watch the sun come up.'

The smile dropped from her face. Firstly she couldn't believe the invitation, secondly it was out of the question. In a plane with only one engine? Never! What chance would one have in an accident if it dropped from the sky? Travelling on roads was bad enough but at least ...'I'm not into that sort of thing. Thanks just the same.'

She made to walk past him, having answered him very pleasantly. His hand on her shoulder came as such a shock, some of her coffee slopped over the side of the mug. The touch of his big, heavy hand seemed to burn right through her housecoat.

'What are you into?' he asked. 'Are you really as bone-idle as you seem?'

'Bone ...? I don't know what you mean.' Kate wrenched her shoulder from his touch. It was beginning to offend her.

He wasn't smiling now. The distaste was back on his face. 'I mean you haven't lifted a finger since you've been here. Three weeks, Kate, you've been here almost three weeks and you haven't cooked a meal, you haven't even put a plate in the dishwasher! I'll bet you haven't peeled a potato, let alone dug some up. Afraid of ruining your nails, are you? You haven't helped with the shopping, I wonder whether you've even offered to help? Can't you *do* something? Would it kill you to milk the goats for Dolly, for example? Pull up a few lettuces and wash them?'

'Now wait a minute——' She stopped abruptly. He simply wasn't worth getting angry with, though she'd like nothing better than to slap his face. 'Adam, she won't let me. She insists I take it easy. Honestly ...' Her voice trailed off. Even as she'd spoken, it had sounded weak to her own ears. It was true that her aunt had refused her help but—but she hadn't insisted, and she felt guilty now. There were plenty of jobs she could have done around the house while Dolly was out.

Nor could she retaliate by accusing Adam of not pulling his weight. He did his share. She had watched him, from the living-room window, chopping wood. Very tall and tanned, shirtless, his perspiring torso glinting in the sunlight. And it was he who tended the fires, he who swept the drive, washed the car.

His brown eyes were hard now, cold. 'Do you know what you are? You're a pathetic excuse for a woman. And what was that about, last night when our neighbours dropped in? You didn't even hang around to be introduced—you fled to your room with the excuse of having a headache—and not for the first time. Because you didn't want to be seen! My God, I've never known such vanity! And the saddest thing of all is that it's mainly in your mind. Of course you're no longer perfect, but your face couldn't offend even if the damage were ten times worse than it is. But that's all there is to you, isn't it? You're just a shell, a doll whose porcelain doll-face has been cracked. Perhaps you are only fit for the rubbish heap. That's what you seem to think, and I'm beginning to agree. There's no more to you, you have nothing left now to offer people. You haven't even got a personality!'

He strode away from her, slamming doors behind him as he left the house.

Kate stood, trembling from head to foot. His words went round and round in her head, provoking such fury she began to feel faint. It was too much. He'd gone too far this time. Why had she stood there, like a fool, coffee cup in hand, taking it? She should have poured the coffee over his head. No personality? Well, he'd see about that. If he so much as spoke to her again, he would rapidly discover she was no empty-headed doll!

Back in her room she paced the floor like an angry tiger. She was high on adrenalin, agitated, wishing Adam were still around so she could punch him in the face. She dragged her hands through her hair, beside herself with a fury she was obliged to contain. What was wrong with her? Why should she let him affect her so? It wasn't as if she cared a hoot for his opinion of her.

She pulled on a pair of jeans and a sweater. For the first time since she'd arrived, she felt the urge to get out. She simply had to. She had to walk. She had to walk off this sudden energy.

Aunt Dolly was in the kitchen, frying bacon. 'Good morning, dear. It's a nice one, isn't it? Not a cloud in the sky! Will you have bacon and eggs with me?'

'No thanks. I—as a matter of fact, I'm going out for a walk.'

'You are?' Her aunt's pleasure was as obvious as her surprise.

Kate forced a smile. 'Yes. I thought I'd take the dogs with me.'

'There's a good girl. That'll save me a job. I want to make an early start today and I've got lots to do yet. It's my meals-on-wheels day, you know.'

The feeling of guilt resurfaced in Kate. Her aunt's gratitude for such a small gesture made her feel awful. Well, Dolly would be in for a few surprises when she got home later on.

Once she was outside with Buster and Bruce lolloping around her, Kate had second thoughts about taking a walk. But the nearest neighbours were several hundred yards away and there wasn't a soul around. She wasn't likely to encounter anyone. The sun had only just come up. There was only the sound of birds for company, an occasional bleat or a moo.

Suddenly she was laughing. The city of London could be on another planet! She walked down the lane at a brisk pace, the dogs going before her, investigating smells in the high hedgerows. Where she was walking, she had no idea, but the dogs would know the way back.

She looked up at the clear blue sky. It was good to be outside! She was alive, alive! No matter what Adam thought, she was alive and there was more to her than a face. The air was cool and crisp and sweet, the animal sounds around her alien and delightful.

When she turned a corner, a solitary rider was coming towards her, a girl on a pony. ''Morning!' she called to Kate.

Kate waved. She wasn't in the habit of greeting or being greeted by strangers, though she thought it nice. Civilised. She returned the greeting—but she was unable to stop herself averting her head.

She walked on.

She felt safe here. The crime rate on Guernsey was very low, she knew, compared to England. Lower than on its sister island, Jersey. And here, out in the country parishes—what danger was there? As for the danger of meeting people—well, if she was to encounter only an occasional rider, she was safe in that respect, too.

She stopped in her tracks, grinning. Before her, by the gateway of someone's property, were bags of vegetables in a little hutch. Beside them was a metal box and a sign scrawled on cardboard. 'Money here, please.'

'How lovely!' she said aloud. How lovely that there still existed places were people trusted people. In any city on the mainland not only would the vegetables vanish, the honesty box would vanish, too! Even the hutch wouldn't be safe.

There were more of them, here and there, flowers in buckets, plants on little stands, bundles of kindling for fires. Kate was delighted. She was out for over an hour—but she did meet someone else. Two people, actually. Two smiling young boys strolling along the lane.

They greeted her, eyeing her speculatively.

'We know who you are!'

'Are you Aunty Dolly's niece? You are, aren't you?'

'She told us you were coming to stay. We came to meet you last week but you were in bed.'

'And it was only half-past five!'

'And Mum and Dad went round last night, and you were in bed again!'

'At seven o'clock! We don't go to bed at seven o'clock. Are you ill?'

Kate help up two hands, laughing. 'Hey, just a minute! I don't believe I caught your names.'

'William.'

'John.'

They were very near one another in age, these two cheerful young souls. About ten and eleven.

'I'm the eldest,' William added, as if reading her thoughts.

'So we're neighbours, are we?' Kate noticed the fuss the dogs were making of them. And judging from their 'Aunty Dolly,' her aunt was very friendly with their parents.

'Where are you off to, school?'

'Yes. We get the bus. What's your name, then?'

'Kate. Kate Sumner.'

'What's happened to your face?' John asked, screwing up his eyes to peer at her.

Kate thought the moment was ruined. She had been revelling in the fact that neither child had looked at her oddly. And now this. But John's next words not only reassured her, they almost made her cry. 'Has Aunty Dolly's cat scratched you?'

'Something like that.' How innocent! she thought. If only that's all there was to it, if only it looked no worse than cat scratches! 'Well, no, I—I was in an accident,

actually.' She could feel herself tensing, hoping the
children weren't going to scrutinise her further.

But William was looking at his watch. '*John!* We've
got to *go*! We'll miss the bus. Come *on*. Cheerie, Kate!'

'Cheerie,' she said. Whatever that meant.

She walked on in the opposite direction. Daffodils
were already in profusion, growing wild on the hedges,
and just as she decided to go back, she took her first
wrong turning and found herself looking at a field of
them.

Mesmerised, she stood and stared. There were
thousands of them, thousands of daffodils bobbing in
the breeze, the sun dappling on their golden-yellow
heads! It was a truly beautiful sight, one that she
wouldn't forget.

As she approached her aunt's house, she turned to
squint up at the sun. It had been at her back as she'd
walked the last stretch. Therefore, the sea was to the
west. Early tomorrow she would walk in the direction
of the sea. It wasn't far away.

Aunt Dolly was just coming out of the house. 'Had a
nice time, Kate? I'm off, but Adam will be back
shortly,' she added, as if it mattered! 'I say, your walk's
put some colour in your cheeks! You look pretty.'

'No,' Kate said grimly. 'Ruddy, yes. Pretty, no way.
Have you got a map of the island? I'd like to see exactly
where this parish is.'

'South-west, dear. You'll find a map inside last year's
telephone directory, in my study. Or should I call it my
office?' She appeared to give this some thought.
'Anyhow, it's the room in which I keep my accounts
and write out cheques!'

The office/study was on the ground floor, next to the
utility rooms. Kate hadn't actually ventured into it
before, she hadn't had reason to. There were hundreds
more books in here. And plants, some free-standing on
the floor or tables, some hanging in baskets from the

ceiling. 'You should call it a library,' she said to her absent aunt. 'Or perhaps a conservatory.' It looked like anything but an office. 'And of course the map is inside last year's telephone directory. I wouldn't expect it to be anywhere else. But *where* is last year's telephone directory?'

She started hunting. Before finding the map she came across a scrapbook, which she flicked open. Press cuttings, it contained press cuttings about Adam. Her eyes moved briefly over the first one . . . Adam Eugene de la Mare, educated at Elizabeth College, Guernsey, he later studied sculpture at Guildford School of Art and at the Royal Academy . . . Examples of his work can be seen in the Brooklyn Museum, the Pennsylvania Academy of Fine Arts, the——

Kate closed the book promptly. She had better things to do!

However, when next she saw Adam, she was civil to him. She had risen above all the nasty things she'd planned on saying. Why stoop to his level, anyway? Cool civility was the best treatment for him. Besides, by then all her anger had been converted to energy she had made good use of. Milking goats and digging up potatoes were things she had no idea how to go about, and going shopping was out of the question, but she could cook well and she was not averse to housework. She spent the morning washing, the afternoon ironing, and her aunt's gratitude added to her feeling of guilt. Well, from now on, she was going to help around the house. Not to gratify *him* but because she wanted to.

CHAPTER THREE

KATE got into the habit of taking an early morning walk. Her leg was better, she could run on it, jump on it, anything. It didn't even ache any more. She loved strolling along the beach, watching the sea, playing with the dogs. At that hour she was safe from strangers (the neighbours' children no longer counted as such). She only saw them if she was late getting up and, apart from her occasional words with them, she saw hardly a soul either on the beach or in the narrow winding lanes around her aunt's house.

Spring was budding all around her and already there were primroses growing in the hedges. Wild, abundant primroses growing so early! Everything seemed to blossom early here. She picked some of them and she bought carnations, iris and freesias very cheaply from the buckets on the lanes. Arranging them in vases and dotting them around the big house was something she took delight in. And it pleased her aunt. 'You have a nice touch,' she said. 'Maybe you should have been a florist instead of a model.'

There had even been a compliment from Adam, not over her flower arrangements but over her cooking. But he paid it unwittingly and, having done so, spoiled everything with that acid tongue of his.

The day her aunt came home with two fresh lobsters, Kate asked if she might cook them. She made Lobster Thermidor, a favourite dish of hers; of everyone, as it turned out.

She watched Adam enjoying the result of her labours. He loved his food, that was something she'd noticed long since. His appetite was voracious compared to hers

41

and yet there was no excess weight on him. He was just—just six feet four and broad!

'Mum, that was absolutely delicious!' he said. He'd been quiet during the meal, even more so than usual, concentrating only on eating. 'What happened to you? You don't normally go in for the exotic—or to such trouble!'

'Nor did I today,' Dolores smiled. 'We have Kate to thank for this. All I did was bring the lobsters home. She's been slaving in the kitchen for hours—wait till you see what's for pud.'

'Well, well, well,' he drawled, looking at Kate, 'so you are good for something, after all.'

Later that evening he resumed the conversation, taking her by surprise as she was sitting in the living-room, reading. Aunt Dolly had gone to bed early and Kate was lost in her book when Adam's voice shattered the silence.

'Talking about being good for something,' he said from the doorway, 'why don't you make yourself really useful and sit for me?'

She had no idea what he meant at first. 'Adam! You frightened the life out of me! I thought you were in your studio.'

'Have you always been such a nervous wreck?'

'No. I mean, I'm not. You startled me, that's all.'

'Perhaps when you've calmed down you'll answer my question?'

She kept her eyes on her book. It was as much as she could do to look at Adam de la Mare, her dislike of him was so intense.

'You're avoiding my eyes again, Kate. So what is your answer?'

'I don't know what your question was.'

'I asked you to sit for me, to model for me. I want to do a bust of you.'

She closed her eyes, fighting for composure. Her fury

with this man had been growing and growing steadily inside her and right now she felt murderous. He wanted to do a bust of her, indeed! Now why on earth would he want to capture her for eternity? Who in their right mind would want to do a head and shoulders of *her*? 'Dear God!' She spoke between gritted teeth. 'You are poison, Adam, poison! Why don't you just leave me alone?'

'Am I to take it that means no?'

'My modelling days are over, you sadistic bastard!'

'Hey! Wait a minute——'

Kate did not wait a minute. She slammed her book shut and marched out, using the door at the other end of the room to make her escape. She was still trembling with anger long after she'd bathed and got into bed.

She didn't see Adam at all the next day, much to her relief. He was around, though. It was Saturday. Aunt Dolly was home for the afternoon and she took some sandwiches and a flask of coffee to him in his studio. She and Kate had theirs in the garden, it was so warm that day. 'Adam was just saying how nice it would be for us to go out to lunch tomorrow, Kate. Lots of the hotels do a splendid Sunday lunch, I'm sure you'd enjoy the change.'

Kate smiled inwardly. Enjoy eating in a public restaurant? Hardly! 'No, I'd rather not, thanks.'

Aunt Dolly didn't push it. 'That's all right, I'm just as happy to do a roast at home.'

Only then did Kate stop to think. This wasn't the first time such a suggestion had been made. 'No! You go, Aunt Dolly. You and Adam. Don't let me stop you.'

'Heavens, no. As I said, I'm just as happy to do my own roast.'

'I'll dig up some potatoes.' Kate was grinning now. Never in her life had she imagined herself doing such tasks, but her aunt had given her quite a few gardening lessons of late. 'And what veges shall we have? Might as well get those, too.'

It was Kate who did the roast the next day—for just the two of them. Adam had announced at breakfast, which they'd all taken together, that he wouldn't be around for lunch. It was another beautiful day and he was going up in his plane.

In the late afternoon, Kate and Dolly looked up as he flew over the house. There were quite a few small aircraft around but his Cessna was distinctive, painted blue and white and flying low. Dolly got to her feet and waved.

'Will he be able to see you?'

'If he's looking, yes!' She was laughing, waving with the vigour she showed in all the things she did.

'Why didn't you go with him?' Kate asked. Adam was probably coming in to land now. He'd said earlier that he was going over to France for the day.

'I wasn't in the mood, dear.' Aunt Dolly sat down again, putting her feet up on the sunbed. Sundays were the only days she did have a rest.

Life went on peacefully for the next few days. Except for Adam, Kate was quite content, content just to potter about the place doing her jobs. His snide remarks kept coming, he never ceased to goad her but she still hung on to her temper.

There was trouble the following Thursday. The evening began well enough. In fact Adam seemed to be quite civilised over dinner.

'Easter's only a couple of weeks away, Adam.' Aunt Dolly was saying. 'Kate's parents are coming over for a few days, and I've been meaning to ask you whether Elena's coming?'

'No, not this year.'

'She's still working in Florence, isn't she?'

'Oh, yes. She's as dedicated as ever.'

Kate felt awkward. She had no idea who Elena was but she hoped her staying away 'this year' was not due to her being there or because her parents were coming to stay.

Adam's next words negated that idea. 'I'm looking forward to seeing your mother, Kate. It's been a long time. She and I get on well, you know. But then Anne must get on with everyone, she's such a nice person. I like your father, too.'

'I—that's nice.' She had no idea why Adam should be chatty with her tonight, but she welcomed it. It was certainly a change to have a civil word from him. She did her best to reciprocate and the atmosphere remained quite pleasant throughout the meal.

'I must dash.' Aunt Dolly glanced at her watch and looked apologetically at Kate. 'I'm sorry to leave you with the clearing up but I have to go, my meeting starts in half an hour.'

Kate hadn't even realised she was going to a meeting. Her aunt had never gone out in the evening before. 'That's all right, all I have to do is stick everything in the dishwasher! When shall I expect you home? I'll have the kettle on for you.'

Aunt Dolly beamed at that. 'You're a good girl, Kate. But I can't say when I'll be back. Adam will look after you, he isn't going out tonight.'

Kate opened her mouth to protest, to laugh, but she caught the wry amusement in Adam's eyes and she said nothing. She wasn't going to leave herself wide open for another attack. She had had a peaceful hour in his presence and she didn't want to spoil things.

When his stepmother left, he said, 'And you had no idea you needed looking after, had you?'

She blinked in surprise. There had been no sarcasm, he really was behaving himself. 'No,' she laughed.

'There's a documentary I want to watch on Channel TV later—if it's all the same to you. I'd watch it upstairs but my telly's on the blink. Must do something about that.'

'I—there's no need for that, Adam. Watch it down here, by all means. It won't disturb me. I can read in Aunt Dolly's study.'

'Why don't you watch the programme with me?'

Suspiciously, she looked straight at him. There was no amusement now, still no sarcasm, he was simply waiting for an answer. 'Well, I . . .' She hardly knew what to say. Having got this far, however, she didn't want him to think she was deliberately avoiding him when he was finally making an effort to be civilised. So she pretended an interest. 'What's it about?'

'Alligators.'

Kate wasn't into alligators but she wasn't going to say so. She'd have shown willing no matter what he wanted to watch. All the time she'd been here, she'd been patient with him and she felt proud of it now. Not once had she lost her temper, though admittedly she'd come very close to it. Her patience seemed to be paying off, it seemed he'd finally got the message that his goading was to no avail. And about time too! Well, it looked as though life might be pleasanter from now on. 'Yes, I'll join you.'

Clearing up in the kitchen, she was bemused, by Adam's apparent friendliness and by a lot of other things. She washed down the work surfaces, taking stock of the weeks she'd spent here. Never in her life would she have believed she could spend night after night indoors and not get bored. There was always something to entertain, if not Dolly's chatter; her stories of how her life used to be when her husband was alive and was a grower of tomatoes, there was always another book waiting to be read. Or there might be a game of Scrabble or cards.

Even during those occasions, when Adam had joined in she had been subject to his barbs. He had made snide remarks about the quiet life she was living, comparing it to the glamour he assumed, rightly, she had known in London, and he had patently not believed her when she claimed she wasn't bored. But she hadn't been. Angered, yes, but not bored.

To her relief, he hadn't always been in during the evening. Half of the time he was in his studio or out somewhere. He never said where he was going, he just went. Kate assumed he went to the aero club or something. To friends, perhaps. From his casual dress, she didn't have the impression he was taking females out. Maybe he was being faithful to Elena? Was she an Italian girlfriend of his?

To her amazement she found that alligators were quite interesting, after all! She was enjoying the documentary—that was, until the advertisements came on. Even before she appeared on the television screen, Kate knew what was coming. The voice-over which started the ad was all too familiar . . .

Then she was looking at herself on the screen, for the first time since the accident. She had made several versions of this advertisement for skin make-up. She hadn't seen any of them while she'd been in hospital or while she'd been here. And now, suddenly, there it was. There *she* was, the camera moving in lovingly for a close-up of her face.

Her face as it used to look.

It was a nasty shock. Kate closed her eyes. She didn't want to see it, didn't want to be reminded of her once-perfect complexion . . .

Adam had started to say something and had stopped talking in mid-sentence. Beyond her closed eyelids, Kate could sense the look she was getting from him. Oh, God. What an awkward moment. For both of them.

She got up swiftly and left the room, muttering, 'Excuse me.' Her heart was thumping with that horrible panic which assailed her at difficult moments and she ran up the stairs and into her room.

Almost immediately there was a knock at the door. Kate, leaning against it, quickly turned the key to lock it. Not now, she had never seen pity in Adam's eyes and she didn't want to see it now. She would rather see his dislike of her than that. 'You—you'll have to excuse me, Adam. I'm——'

'Open the door.'

'No, I'm—I don't want to watch the rest of the programme.'

'To hell with the programme! I said open this door!' Suddenly he was booming at her, his voice was so loud and angry it made her jump even though she was protected by inches of solid wood.

'Adam, please, leave me alone. I'm—I can't face——' Her voice trembled to a halt. She wanted to say she couldn't stand a scene with him, not another, not now. Oh, God, not now, when she was so very vulnerable.

'Can't face what?' he roared. 'Me or yourself? Can't stand the sight of yourself either way, can you? Can't stand seeing the way you used to look, can't stand the way you look today! You're a coward, Kate, a pathetic little coward!'

Coward? Kate unlocked the door and flung it open. 'Coward? Coward! What the hell would you know? Have you any conception of what I've been through? Have you——'

'Shut up!' He cut through her protests furiously. 'For God's sake stop feeling sorry for yourself and listen to me——'

'Out, get *out* of here. I'm sick of you, I've had as much as I can stand from you and now you've gone too far! You're crazy. How dare you call me a coward? You're the last person on this earth who could understand how I felt just now——'

Adam ignored that. He grabbed hold of both her arms and shoved her on to the bed, roaring so loudly she began to feel really frightened. 'If you don't shut up and listen to me, I'm going to paddle your behind until you beg for mercy. You have the nerve to tell me you're sick of me? Well hear this, you broken little doll, *I'm* sick of *you*. If things don't start changing around here, I personally will stuff you in a trunk and throw you off the island. Have you got that?'

Kate was dumbstruck. She was beginning to think he'd gone off his rocker. Her eyes moved swiftly to the door.

'It's no use doing that. Dolly's not in, remember? She's not here to protect you from me, to protect you from the *truth*. I wonder if you have any idea how much you're upsetting this household? Do you realise my stepmother hasn't had an evening out in weeks? She's only gone out tonight because she had to. Have you stopped to ask yourself why? It's because she won't leave you on your own. And we all know you won't come out, don't we? You're absolutely neurotic, Miss Sumner, and you have the nerve to accuse me of being crazy!'

Kate put her hands over her ears. The fight had drained out of her. Was it true? Had her aunt stayed in because—because she was babysitting her? 'Why—why are you saying this? I don't believe you! Aunt Dolly wouldn't——'

'Aunt Dolly would. Aunt Dolly does. She feels that one or other of us has to be around. She's worried about you, you moron, don't you know that? She's worried by your behaviour. You dress like a tramp, you hardly ever have your nose out of a book, you've inhibited our neighbours from calling and the only time you leave this house is in the early hours, when you think you won't be seen. What's it all about, that's what I want to know. Why do you continue to hide? Because you've got a few marks on your face?'

'Don't give me that! You saw me on TV just now. You saw how I used to look——'

'I know how you used to look.' He was still shouting at her. He was frightening her and she was confused, thinking about her aunt, wondering if it were true, if

Dolores were really so worried. 'I know a great deal about you, Kate, more than you realise. I know what's been going through your mind, too. I know about your fears, your frustrations.'

Oh, did he really? She saw red at that. Everything else was forgotten for the moment as her emotions see-sawed. She flung herself off the bed and lashed out at him viciously. '*You?* You couldn't begin to understand! Try, just try to imagine how you'd feel if something happened to rob you of your career—if you had an accident which damaged those talented hands of yours. How do you think you'd cope?' She lost control. In the next instant she was lunging at him, battering her fists against his chest. She wanted to kill him.

'Kate! Kate, stop that.' Suddenly his voice was quiet. It was easy enough for him to stop her flailing hands. He caught hold of both her arms and pinned them to her sides, looking straight at her. 'I don't know,' he said softly, incredibly softly, his eyes closing as he spoke.

Kate stood motionless in his grip, staring at him.

'I don't know,' he said again. He opened his eyes to look straight into hers. 'I don't know what I'd do, Kate. But I can imagine how you feel, believe it or not.'

She didn't believe it. Not for one minute. A great, shuddering sigh escaped from her and she went limp the moment he released his grip. 'Get out of here,' she said dully. 'I'll talk to Dolly tomorrow and sort things out—make it clear that I don't need a babysitter—you or her.'

'Kate, I want——'

'I'm not interested,' she said wearily. 'Just go, I've had as much as I can take in one night.'

Adam hesitated a second, seemingly giving thought to the remark. 'Then I'll talk to you tomorrow. I haven't finished with you yet. And there's something I want to show you. Sooner or later I'm going to knock some sense into you.'

His words hung on the air like the threat that they
were. Tiredly, Kate closed the door, which he'd left
wide open, locked it, stripped off and got into bed
without even cleaning her teeth. She felt drained,
emotionally worn out. But she was not, she was *not*
going to go home. Even Adam de la Mare was a better
prospect than her mother's weepy sympathy or her
friends' lack of interest.

No, she would leave this house only if her aunt asked
her to, which wasn't likely. Oh, but she felt guilty!
Adam had been right in some of the things he'd said.
She had disturbed the household, she had been
thoughtless and selfish. Why Dolly imagined she needed
someone to keep an eye on her, she didn't know. But it
wouldn't do. She realised now why her aunt had
pretended disinclination to go flying with Adam—when
really she loved it. And there was the business of going
out for a meal . . . of not going out. Because of Kate.

Tomorrow, she would talk to Aunt Dolly tomorrow.

It was ten minutes to ten when Kate woke up the next
day. She looked groggily, stupidly, at clock by her bed.
But was it any wonder she'd slept so late? She hadn't
fallen asleep till almost four in the morning. Her mind
had been spinning with all that had happened, going
round and round in circles.

She got out of bed, still feeling tired, and hoped Aunt
Dolly would be around. What day was this? Friday.
Was it Dolly's hospital visiting day today?

It was. Dolores was out. She had left a note by the
kettle for Kate, and when she read it, she panicked. She
made a mug of tea and took it back to her room,
wondering what she was going to do. All her aunt had
asked for was a simple favour but it was more than
Kate could cope with.

Half an hour later she was walking down the field

towards Adam's studio, having rehearsed what she was
going to say.

It was the end of March and she was venturing into
his studio for the first time. It proved to be an
unforgettable day for Kate. She ended up wishing she
had never been born. She didn't want to trespass on
Adam's domain, didn't want to disturb him, didn't even
want to speak to him, but she had no choice. She was in
a state of panic, not that she would let him know it.

From the middle of March the weather had turned
warm and it stayed warm. On this particular morning it
was raining, not that Kate noticed. In jeans and a T-
shirt she hurried across the fields and knocked on the
door of the studio. When there was no answer she let
herself in. Then she laughed.

It was one enormous room, so big that he wouldn't
have heard her knock.

Her eyes scanned it rapidly but there was no sign of
him. What she did see made her gasp in admiration. It
was almost too much to take in. She advanced slowly
into the middle of the room. There, standing on the
ground on a wooden base board, was a life-size model
of a young girl; one arm was shyly covering her breasts,
which it did only partially, and the hand of her other
arm was modestly covering her pubic area. Kate stared
at it, her panic totally if only temporarily forgotten.

The model was not only beautiful, it seemed to be
alive! Adam had captured precisely the girl's embarrassment, in her stance, her facial expression, in her
eyes. Kate identified with it immediately, though
physically it was nothing like her. She had been that
girl, once. Every woman had been that girl once. With
budding breasts, hips which had just begun delicately to
curve and with a painful shyness at being caught naked.

She stepped away from it, enjoying it from all angles.
It was modelled from clay and it was unfinished. The
feet had yet to take shape.

And there were other models in the making. Kate looked round, fascinated, at armatures of various shapes and sizes. So that was how it all began, with a metal frame on to which the clay, or plaster or whatever the medium, was built.

She looked up at the high ceiling. It had been apparent on looking at this one-time stable block from her bedroom window that the roof had big glass panels in it but she hadn't realised that the north-facing wall was one vast sheet of glass. Against another wall there were two sinks, a big marble slab on either side of them. Beside those there were rows and rows of shelves filled with neatly labelled bottles and jars: beeswax, turpentine, methylated spirit, ammonia, Venetian soap, caustic soda, linseed oil—the list went on. On the floor there were differently coloured bins with numbers written on their lids. Clay? Plaster of Paris? The numbers told her nothing.

Her exploration went on and as she took it all in, she knew a sneaking regard for Adam, an unwilling respect. As she became aware of this, she glanced again at the young girl. Yes, his talent was enormous and somewhere, somehow, there had to be a great deal of sensitivity in him. There just had to be, he couldn't have understood the girl's feelings so precisely if there weren't. She only wished it showed outside his work—outside his studio!

The rest of the work in progress was almost wholly of the human form. Or would be, judging from the shapes of the armatures. On another rack of shelves there were plaster casts of arms and legs, in front of the big window was a drawing board; on it and on a nearby table there were sketches, dozens of them, different subjects but all people. On another table, placed neatly in rows, were Adam's tools. Kate could name some of them, chisels, mallets, wirecutters, spatulas and something which looked suspiciously like a cheese grater!— but most of them looked like tools a dentist might use.

'Yes, Kate?'

At the sound of his voice, curt, gravelly and unwelcoming, she spun round. There was a door at the opposite end of the studio she hadn't even noticed. 'I—I didn't realise—what's in there?'

He was advancing on her rapidly. 'A darkroom. I don't think I need to tell you to keep out.'

No he didn't, any more than he need to tell her he wanted her out of his studio. Kate glanced again at the girl in the centre of the room, the urge to pay him a compliment dying in her throat. A. E. de la Mare's sculptures fetched vast sums of money; he didn't need her to tell him he was good. 'Look, I'm sorry to disturb you——'

'That makes two of us.' He was level with her now, hands shoved into the pockets of his filthy smock, looking down at her with that disconcerting directness. 'I'd planned on talking to you later.'

'This is hardly a social visit.' She kept her voice reasonable, having no wish to irritate him further.

'So what do you want?'

She looked away. Heavens, he was so easy to hate! But she had to be careful if she were to get her own way. 'Aunt Dolly left me a note and a shopping list. She wants me to go into the village. Er—she says there's a supermarket there.'

'So you want the keys to the pick-up?'

'Actually, no. I—I wondered if you wouldn't mind going?' She dug into the pocket of her jeans and pulled out the shopping list.

Adam ignored her outstretched hand. He moved away from her, leaning against a sink, his arms folded across his massive chest now. 'Why?'

'Because the only means of transport is your pick-up, and I'm sure you won't like the idea of my driving it on these narrow roads.'

'Why?'

'Well . . .' What an awkward devil he was! Still, she maintained her friendly approach and flashed her very best smile at him. 'I've—I've never driven such a big vehicle before.'

'It's the same as driving a car, it's just a bit bigger. The gears are the same. The keys are in the ignition, help yourself.'

'Well, to be honest,' she said, with a little laugh, determined not to be beaten, 'I'd never find my way to the village and back!'

'Why? Are you stupid?'

'Adam——'

'You've got a tongue in your head, haven't you? If you take a wrong turning, you can ask directions.'

'Adam, please——' She hated herself as much as she hated him in that moment, for having to appeal to him like this. 'The truth is, I haven't driven since the accident and—I think I've lost my nerve.'

He was unmoved. 'All the more reason to get behind a wheel as quickly as possible, I'd say. But that isn't the truth, Kate. Who do you think you're kidding? Why don't you admit you're a coward, that you're scared?'

'Look, I am telling you the truth! I'd get well and truly lost and the pick-up truck is daunting and there's no way I can handle it on these narrow little lanes! All I'm asking is a favour.'

'And the answer is no. Besides, you could walk it at a pinch.' His eyes travelled slowly, insolently, over the length of her body as she stood facing him, just two yards away. 'Perhaps not. It would be a bit much for a city girl.'

Kate finally lost her temper—good and proper. 'Oh, for God's sake, stop it! Stop it! I have no idea why you take such delight in putting me down. I've been more than patient with you and I've always been civil to you. I don't know what I've done to make you hate me but I'm up to here with you! I've had enough. All right, I'm

scared, scared! Is that what you want me to admit? I
don't want to face people! I can't bear the way they
look at me! I am *not going* to the supermarket. On foot
or in any other fashion. And unless you're prepared to
go without your flasks of coffee today, you can damn
well buy some yourself because we've run out!' Her face
was red again and she hated herself for it. What had
happened to the cool, collected girl she used to be? And
this was all so stupid—so much fuss over nothing!

Adam de la Mare took one stride towards her and
Kate froze, her heart thumping. He looked so—so
menacing, she didn't know what to expect. His heavy
hands dropped like clamps on her shoulders. 'So you
have got a tongue in your head! So there *is* a bit of
character in you! So you're *not* just a pretty face!'

There was no time for thought. Blinded by an
unprecedented rage, Kate all but screamed at him. 'You
bastard! By God, you really know how to hurt, don't
you?' She wrenched away from him frantically and ran,
blinded by tears now.

Adam caught up with her in no time. 'Wait!' He
caught hold of her arm and stopped her in her tracks,
spinning her round to face him. Kate's arm was already
in mid-air, she had stood for far too much from this
man, for too long. She landed a very hard and very
satisfying slap across his face. Because he was so taken
by surprise, she wrenched free again—almost.

Almost. He held on to her wrist. 'Come here, you
idiot, I want to explain——'

She couldn't see at all now. He was just a blur
through her tears. But she heard. 'Get away from me!'
She was actually screaming now, wriggling and fighting
like someone demented. She'd stood enough, more than
enough! 'You're a sadistic, hateful *beast*. I said let *go*
of——'

It happened at that precise instant. How, quite, she
wasn't sure. All she knew was that one minute she was

pulling and he was pulling, her arms were flying, her booted foot landed against his shin and then her body slammed against something solid—and it wasn't Adam.

There was an almighty crash.

Then there was stillness. For split seconds everything seemed to happen in slow motion. She was still, he was still, and the model of the young girl was falling, falling ... Its invisible metal frame tore free from its supports and in the next instant it was a heap of cracked and battered clay on the floor.

Kate didn't think of looking at Adam for a reaction. All she saw was hours and hours of work in a pile of destruction—and she ran, petrified. She ran like hell, out of the studio, across the fields, into the house, up the stairs ...

Even behind her locked bedroom door she didn't feel safe. She was right not to. She held her breath.

Silence.

There was total silence.

She leaned against the wall, panting for air, and let herself slide to the floor. She was shaking from head to foot. 'Oh, God!' She bowed her head against her knees, muttering to herself. 'Oh, God, how awful! How *awful*!' That beautiful statue ... Telling herself that its destruction was the fault of its creator was no consolation at all. She had to share the responsibility. If she hadn't kicked him so hard on the shin ... Worse, she couldn't help feeling she had robbed the world of something glorious. In her mind's eye she could still see the girl, she could see the sculpture finished, cast, magnificent in bronze ...

In reality she saw the door handle turning. Her hand flew to her mouth at the sound of Adam's voice.

'Open the door, Kate.'

There was no chance of her doing that. His voice was like ice and she was terrified by it. It was too calm to be true. She uttered not one sound, all she could think of was the tragedy of the model and the fury he must be feeling now. Her hands were shaking uncontrollably.

The cold, unnaturally calm voice came at her again. 'I'm going to count to three before I kick the door open. One . . .'

Kate crawled out of the way on hands and knees. She stared at the solid wood door and at the lock, praying it would hold.

There followed an enormous thud as Adam's foot connected with the door. The lock surrendered easily and it slammed back on its hinges . . .

CHAPTER FOUR

KATE couldn't move. She looked up at Adam as he towered over her and was convinced he was going to strike her. She could see in his eyes all the fury he was entitled to be feeling. There were no excuses. Though she'd stood for so much from him for so long, she felt guilty. She couldn't get that sculpture out of her mind, and the hours and hours of work he'd put in to it. 'I'm sorry,' she said quickly. 'I'm very sorry about the model, I can't tell you how much . . .'

'Get up.' He spoke with that same icy hardness he'd used before kicking her door open. 'Get off the floor, I want to talk to you.'

She couldn't. She didn't have the strength. Her legs were like jelly. 'I can't.'

He muttered something she didn't catch. Two seconds later she was being lifted bodily and deposited on a chair. Adam sat on the edge of the bed, arms folded, looking at her. Very quietly he said, 'My patience with you has just run out.'

Patience? He didn't know the meaning of the word. 'Adam, please, I—it was an accident!' She was trembling, afraid to look at him. 'I'm sorry, sorry, sorry!'

'Forget the sculpture. It doesn't matter. Look at me. *Look at me.*'

She couldn't do that either. His calmness was terrifying. The very air was reverberating with his unspoken fury.

'I—I'm too scared.'

'Of what?'

'Of you. What else?'

'There are lots of things you're afraid of but I don't
think I'm one of them. At least I hope not. My friends
call me the gentle giant, Kate.' He almost purred at her
as if to convince her. 'How could anyone be frightened
of me? I'm just a great big pussy cat.'

Kate went rigid. Her head came up and tears
streamed down her face. His voice, the very stillness
of his body was menacing. He was going to pounce
any second, she knew it, she was not fooled by the
outward calmness. 'I'll leave,' she whispered. 'If you'll
just—please—leave me alone, I'll pack my cases.
Now.'

'You're not leaving. You're not going anywhere other
than the shops. For today.'

'I—the shops? What are you talking about?'

'I'd have thought that was plain enough. You, we,
are going to the village to get Dolly's shopping.
Tomorrow you are going into Town with me. On
Sunday you, your aunt and I are going out to lunch.
There will be no arguments, no more hysterics. You will
do as I say until such time as I decide to leave you to
your own devices.'

Even before she spoke, Kate knew with absolute
certainty that this was indeed how it was going to be.
But she tried. 'I—there are some things you can't do to
me, Adam. You can humiliate me, insult me, reduce me
to tears, but you can't make me go out if I don't want
to.'

Slowly, he got to his feet and walked over to where
she sat. The fingers of his left hand closed around her
upper arm. He didn't speak. His face was implacable.
He used no force at all, he didn't need to. Like a
zombie, Kate got up and allowed him to guide her to
her bathroom. Her heart was knocking against her ribs
like a sledgehammer. There was, she knew, no way she
would change his mind. She was afraid even to try
again, she felt as if she were being held by a time-bomb.

Any minute now he could explode and—she dreaded to think about that.

'Wash those tears away,' he said softly. 'I'm not affected by weeping women. Never have been.'

All sorts of things flashed through her mind while she was in the bathroom, silly ideas. She looked at the closed door and thought of locking herself in. But that wouldn't work. She looked at the window and thought of climbing out. But it was a long way down to the gravel driveway. Instead she washed her face, combed her hair and resigned herself.

Adam was on the landing where she'd left him, leaning against the wall. He took hold of her arm again. 'Come along, Kate,' he said, as if she were six years old. 'There's a good girl.'

A million butterflies were jumping around in her stomach and it was not only at the prospect of facing a supermarket. As she walked down the stairs at Adam's side, she glanced at him and felt she was seeing a stranger. What had happened to him? She had seen him in many moods but she'd never known anything like this.

He led her to the pick-up truck, opened the passenger door and waited while she climbed in. 'You can stop trembling now, Kate. This isn't going to be half as bad as you expect. Nobody is going to stare at you, I guarantee it. Except, of course, if there are some men around. Then you might be looked at—but they'll be stares of appreciation.'

As he got behind the driving wheel he said, 'Here, allow me.' He leaned over and fastened her safety belt for her. She was trying to do it herself but her hands were shaking so much, she couldn't. Then he did and said something odd. He looked at her and smiled. 'As a matter of interest, seat belts aren't compulsory in Guernsey.' He put the palm of his hand against her cheek, touching her scars with infinite gentleness, and added, 'But there's no law against wearing them, either.'

Kate was speechless. She didn't know what to make of him. After all these weeks she had come to rely on his cruelty and now—now he was frightening her with gentleness! It was as if he knew precisely what she was thinking, feeling.

Staring straight ahead of her and wanting to be sick, she looked neither left nor right on the way to the village of St Pierre du Bois. It had stopped raining now. In no time at all, Adam was parking the truck between two cars in the car park outside a supermarket. There was also a dry cleaner's and a bank. 'Off you go, Kate. I'll wait here for you. I hate shopping for food.'

If she could have known how pathetically she looked at him, how meek she sounded, she'd have been ashamed of herself. 'I—don't want to go in there, Adam.'

'I know that.'

'Please, will you at least come with me?'

'No.'

She slumped in her seat.

'Go, Kate.'

'I—didn't pick up my bag. I haven't got any money.' She turned her head away and found herself looking at an Alsatian in the car parked next to them. She felt her hand being lifted and she turned to see Adam pressing a wad of notes into it. 'I haven't got the shopping list, either.' Nor had she, she'd lost it in the scuffle.

Adam pulled it from his trouser pocket. It was a screwed-up ball of paper which he flattened out on his knee. 'Here you are!' he said cheerfully. 'I rescued it for you! Now . . .' The ridiculous cheerfulness vanished. '. . . have you finished playing for time?'

Kate opened the door and got out. She had no choice. 'I hate you, Adam.' She hissed at him through the open window. 'I hate the sight of you!'

He smiled at that. 'I'll tell you what I'll do. When you

come back, I'll give you five pounds for anyone who's stopped and looked at you twice. I'll do that if it happens here or anywhere else.'

'Then you'd better have a lot more cash on you.' She was shaking again.

Adam waited until she'd got half way across the car park before shouting to her. 'Kate! Wait a minute.'

She stopped in her tracks, feeling not only self-conscious but also idiotic as two women turned to look at her. Did he have to bellow like that? 'What now?' She snapped at him as he approached her.

He shook his head in exaggerated sadness. 'Dear me, you look so sorry for yourself, walking at a snail's pace like that, as if you're going to your doom. I think you'd better have this, to take your mind off yourself.' And with that, he put both arms around her and lifted her clean off the floor, bringing his mouth down to hers at the same time. He kissed her long and hard, keeping her suspended in mid-air so she was helpless to fight him.

When he dropped her back on her feet, she couldn't believe what had happened. Her mouth opened and closed twice. Nothing came out. From the corner of her eye she could see the two women—just standing, watching.

Unable to find her voice, Kate bolted into the supermarket.

Half an hour later, she emerged.

And she was smiling.

Adam was smiling, too. He got out of the truck, took the plastic shopping bags from her and stuck them in the back. He said nothing until Kate was seated. 'Well? How much do I owe you?'

'I—n-n-nothing. Nothing!' She burst into tears.

With a sigh, Adam put an arm around her and pulled her gently against him. He let her cry, stroking the black silk of her hair as he waited for her to find her voice.

At length she pulled away from him, hardly able to look him in the face. 'You were right. You were right! Nobody took any notice of me but——'

'But what?'

For a man who claimed to be unaffected by women's tears, he'd been remarkably gentle with her and not only did she feel foolish, she was embarrassed at the way she had allowed him to hold her, the way she had cried on his shoulder. Defiantly she finished what she was saying. 'But I hate your methods, Adam. I've done what you wanted me to do but I'll never forgive you for the way you forced me into it.'

He shrugged, started the engine. 'The end justifies the means.'

'Like hell it does.'

She watched the scenery on the way home, secretly joyous because it was true, nobody had looked at her oddly, let alone with pity. She couldn't understand it.

Back at the house, she put the groceries away and all the time she was doing so, Adam was leaning against the fridge, watching her.

She filled the kettle. 'I suppose you'll have a cup of coffee now we've got some?'

'Yes, please, Kate. That's very kind.'

His unprecedented politeness shook her. She felt insecure, not knowing where she was with him. 'What now? Why are you watching me as if I'm a specimen under glass?'

There was no answer.

'I don't like the way you're looking at me, Adam, and I don't like being your victim. And what was all that about, in the car park?'

Again there was no answer. He let his eyes roam over her from head to toe, let them linger deliberately on the swell of her breasts in the T-shirt. 'You have beautiful breasts,' he said, as if he were familiar with them. 'I wish you'd model for me. I'd like to do you life-size.'

Her guilt resurfaced. 'Adam—about the girl, the sculpture. I—I'm——'

'Forget it.' He shrugged. He merely shrugged. 'I wasn't satisfied with her anyway. She was too damned perfect to be true.'

Kate frowned, unable to believe that. 'Even I know that clay can be re-shaped! Just because you weren't satisfied——'

'I don't want to hear another word about it.' Adam pushed himself away from the fridge. 'Bring the coffee down to the studio in the flask. We'll drink it there.'

'No. I don't want——'

He turned, tiredly, uninterestedly. 'I no longer care what you want. You'll do as you're told. Have you forgotten what I told you earlier? You're under my orders until I free you from them. Besides,' he added, a sudden smile lighting up his eyes, 'I've got something to show you.'

That was the only reason Kate went to the studio. She stood, not knowing what she was going to do about him, after he'd gone. He couldn't order her around! What did he have to show her? She couldn't imagine. And it wasn't the first time he'd mentioned it. Curiosity got the better of her.

Adam was just emerging from his darkroom when she got to the studio. 'Put the flask on the table,' he said, 'and sit down. No, not there, at the big table by the window.'

Kate's curiosity was soon satisfied. Adam spread before her a batch of newly developed photographs. Photographs of *her*. She couldn't believe it. From the sweater she was wearing in them, she knew they'd been taken yesterday. There she was, picking primroses from a hedge. There she was again, on the beach with the dogs. And again, sitting on a rock. And again and again. There were more than a dozen of them. 'Adam! How—what . . .? I don't understand.'

He drew up a chair and sat next to her. 'They were taken with a zoom lens.'

'I realise that! Cameras hold no mystery for me, you know. But why? Why did you—you must have followed me!'

'Obviously.' He was brisk, business-like. He opened a folder which was on the table and watched the expression on her face.

The first photo in the folder had been taken several days ago. It had also been taken with a zoom lens, as had the newer ones. 'I've told you, I plan to do a sculpture of you. With or without the live model.' He was watching her closely. 'But it's occurred to me that these photos can serve another purpose. You've taken a big step forward today, Kate, but I wonder if you're really convinced? So look at this.' He flipped to the back of the folder and drew from a plastic covering a close-up photograph of her face.

Kate stared at it. In the picture, she was asleep. In the armchair in the house. Her head was slightly to one side and the bruise on her cheekbone, all the damage in the area, was startlingly plain to see. She looked from the photograph to the photographer, recoiling from him. Very quietly, she said, 'I think you'd better explain yourself. This is sick, sick! What the devil are you up to?'

'Don't be so dramatic. I've already told you why I've photographed you.' He glanced round the studio, spotted what he wanted and got up. 'Don't move.'

She had no thought of moving, she was staring again with incredulity at the horrible close-up of herself.

Adam was back. With a mirror. 'Look at yourself.'

'I'd rather——' She took the mirror. There was, she knew only too well, no point in trying to defy this man. She looked. 'So?'

There was plenty of light in the studio but even so,

Adam switched on the spotlight on the table. He turned it so it was aimed straight at her face.

'So?' she said again.

He got up, moved to the back of her chair and gathered all her hair into his hands. 'Take a long, hard look, Kate.'

She did.

'And now look at this.' He placed in her hand the photo she'd just been staring at. It was one of the earliest ones he'd taken, when she had been at the house only a few days.

The difference was—unbelievable! Kate looked from the photograph to her reflection again and again, and tears started trickling from her eyes.

Adam stayed where he was, standing behind her chair. He put an arm around her shoulders and took the mirror from her, holding it in front of her. Then he let his hand slide up to her neck, to her chin, tilting it upwards so they could both see her reflection. 'You see,' he said softly. 'I didn't lie when I said you're not just a pretty face. Look again, Kate. You're still beautiful, after all.'

That was a gross exaggeration but—but still! In her gratitude she reached for his hand without thinking and clung to it tightly. 'Th-thank you. I—I just didn't realise . . .'

'How much you've healed?' She couldn't see him now but there was no mistaking the sorrow in his voice. 'That's because you haven't looked. Oh, you see yourself daily in a mirror but you haven't really looked. All you've seen are the flaws. All you've thought about is the way you used to look. And when your reflection didn't live up to that, you remained blinkered. You've been managing somehow to see your face as it was when you first got here. But that's six weeks ago, nature has played her part since then.' He threw the photograph on to the table and sat down again, facing her, a wry smile on his mouth. 'Isn't it odd how the mind works, Kate? Your face is not perfect, not flawless, but it's lovely nonetheless. And you can see it for yourself now. You had nothing to be frightened of, going into the supermarket. I wouldn't have bet money otherwise!'

She couldn't make a joke of it. The tears were still streaming silently from her, she'd never felt so happy, so hopeful, in her life.

'In my opinion,' Adam went on quietly, 'you're as beautiful now as you were before. You'll accuse me of being perverse, I've no doubt, but I don't know—perhaps it's because of the imperfection. I can see you don't believe me.' He shrugged. 'Well, whatever my faults, Kate, I'm not a liar. I might be a sadist, I might be all the other things you've accused me of being, but I'm not a liar. I do think you're beautiful, and I have no reason at all to flannel you, have I?'

In the ensuing silence, Kate was unable to take her eyes from him. Already her head was held higher. His brown eyes matched her scrutiny, letting her see that he'd told the truth. 'No. No, you haven't.'

He seemed gratified by that. 'How about some coffee?'

She poured it into two blue mugs he fetched from the sink, one of which had no handle on it. 'I wish Aunt Dolly would come home,' she said, thinking aloud. 'I've got to apologise to her.'

'There's no need for that. Your going out will be her reward. You see, Kate, what you don't know is—well, your mother has been so upset, she thought you might try to do something stupid.'

'Something——' As she realised what he meant, she was horrified. 'Good grief! So that's why you and Dolly have been keeping an eye on me! Oh, no,' she added grimly. 'There's no way I'd take my life, ever, don't worry about that!'

'I never did. It was the women who worried. Your mother couldn't let you know quite how concerned she's been. Reassurances haven't washed with you. You've been impossible to get through to.'

But he'd got through to her. Her smile was wry. 'You managed.' She sighed, rubbing tiredly at her eyes. What a day it had been! 'And I'm grateful to you.' She glanced again at the photos he had taken without her knowledge. 'I don't like your methods, I think you're the hardest, most insensitive person I've ever met, but I am grateful to you for making me see things as they really are.' She got wearily to her feet. 'Please excuse me now, I need to be alone for a while.'

Adam nodded, making no comment, no attempt to stop her.

Back in her bedroom, Kate looked at her reflection in the mirror. She looked closely, long and hard, which was something she had avoided doing for weeks. Only now did it register that the bruise had vanished long since, that the patchwork of tiny scars were healing very satisfactorily. The surgeon who had repaired her shattered cheekbone and stitched her up had done wonders. There was no redness now, even. 'And who knows,' she asked aloud, a new joy in her heart, 'maybe the plastic surgery will restore me completely!'

She hadn't dared to hope for that before. She had been told there would be no guarantees, but . . . and yet somehow it didn't seem all that important now, for some reason. She looked at herself again and again, holding her hair back, as Adam had. It was true, she was still attractive. Not perfect, not beautiful, but attractive!

CHAPTER FIVE

'GET behind the wheel, Kate.'

'But——'

'*Behind the wheel.* You're driving.'

She did as he ordered but she was still protesting. As far as she knew, they were going to the village to collect some dry cleaning for Dolores. 'When you said you were coming with me, I thought you meant you were giving me a lift.'

'Did you indeed? Why should I chauffeur you around?'

'If you're not doing the driving, what's the point in your coming with me?'

Adam climbed into the passenger seat. 'It seems there's no end to my kindness, doesn't it?'

There was no answer to that. Kate threw him a filthy look and turned the key in the ignition.

Late last night she had stood by her window for ages, looking at the lights from the studio and thinking. Aunt Dolly had been delighted on hearing she had braved the supermarket—and she'd unwittingly told Kate that she had left the note and the shopping list *on Adam's instructions*!

'So it worked!' she'd exclaimed, delighted. 'Adam said if I asked a special favour of you, it might get you out of the house. How clever of him!'

Dumbstruck, Kate had stared at Dolores in disbelief. But not for long. It was all perfectly clear, really; Adam de la Mare was a crafty, cunning, conniving ... 'But— oh, dear!' Frustrated, she'd tried to explain how terrible the day had been. 'Aunt Dolly, it wasn't as simple as that. I—Adam and I had an awful fight during the morning.'

'Don't be silly, dear. You mean you had a row, I suppose!'

Kate had kept an eye on the kitchen door throughout the conversation. She didn't want Adam walking in. Aunt Dolly hadn't seen him yet and she didn't want her to get his version of the story first. 'No, I mean a fight, an awful, physical fight!'

'Good grief! What on earth was it about?'

'I——' Kate groaned inwardly. If she'd had any inkling that Adam had plotted the way he had, she'd have ignored her aunt's note completely. 'The shopping, of course. I didn't want to go.'

'But all's well that ends well, dear. Why worry now?'

'Because—because there was a terrible accident.' She went on to tell Dolores everything, well almost everything, that had happened. At length she said, 'I feel so guilty, when I think about that beautiful sculpture . . . I don't believe Adam isn't upset. He must be. He must hate me.'

'What nonsense! Adam hasn't got it in him to hate anybody. He's such a dear, sweet man. How can you think that?'

What was the point? What was the point, really?

Now, Kate glanced at the 'dear, sweet man' in the pick-up truck beside her. She wasn't exactly at her best this morning and she was about to drive for the first time since the accident, a strange vehicle at that, *and* on those impossibly narrow lanes!

'Well?' he demanded. 'What are we waiting for?'

Kate switched the engine off. 'Adam, there's something I want to you to know. Dolores told me it was your idea she should leave that note yesterday.'

'That's right.' He smiled, dismissing the subject.

'But——'

'You're doing it again,' he accused, 'playing for time. Or trying to.' He leaned over and switched the engine on again. 'Let's go, woman, let's go!'

'I—you're impossible. Do you know that? *Impossible*.'
Kate slammed the gear lever into first. 'I can't imagine
why you drive this horrid thing, why don't you drive a
car like everyone else? A small one, preferably! You'll
have to direct me, I've already forgotten which way to
go.' They moved off with a jerk.

'Hey, take it easy, will you? Have some consideration
for the clutch! I happen to be very fond of this truck.
Now then, when you get to the lane, turn left, then left
again, right, then left again, right, right, left again——'

'*Adam!*'

He threw back his head and roared with laughter. Kate
almost drove into the gate post. She had never heard
him laugh before, it was like the rumble of an
earthquake, fascinating on the ears as well as the eyes.

It was a long time before she realised he was leading
her a dance. Once they were out of the immediate
vicinity of the house, she was totally lost. They passed a
church which she knew was not St Peter's and then, a
few miles later, another one. 'Where are we? We
should've reached the village by now!'

'The village?' He looked blank. 'We're going to
Town.'

Kate put the brakes on. Oh, no, she wasn't going to
drive the entire width of the island in this vehicle. She
told him so.

'Why, Kate! You're beginning to sound like a local!
It's all of six or seven miles from one side of this island
to the other! The whole package is only twenty-four
square miles. One day, if you're very good indeed, I'll
let you drive the entire *length* of the island! For the time
being, get on with the task in hand. I told you yesterday
you were coming to Town with me.'

Exasperated, she threw up her hands. 'I thought we
were collecting the dry cleaning!'

'We are. On the way back. Now get going and don't
be so soft. Town first, then the Bridge.'

'The Bridge?'

'St Sampson's to you.' Adam shook his head at her. 'Drive on, we're almost there.'

They went down into St Peter Port on Le Val des Terres, the steepest, curliest road she'd seen in her life. 'You've done this on purpose, too,' she accused. 'There must be another route into Town.'

'There is. But this is the most difficult road on the island. Some say.'

Just as he spoke, they rounded the last bend and Kate had her first look at St Peter Port harbour, and a very pretty sight it was. 'I hate you,' she muttered. 'I think the island is lovely but if you are typical of Guernsey people, I'm not going to like them at all.'

'Yes, Kate.'

'And another thing—I do not like being conned.'

'No, Kate.'

Catching sight of some islands off the coast, she exclaimed in delight. 'How lovely! What are those islands?'

'Jethou and Herm. And the one further out is Sark. I'm going to take you over to see them next week, weather permitting. Now watch this roundabout, it's tricky. Look out for traffic from the right.'

'Where are we going to park?'

'That's a very good question. I'll make it as awkward as I can for you.'

She didn't think he was joking. She was right. Her hands were trembling by the time she'd squeezed the pick-up between two Minis on one of the piers. Ah, but she was pleased with herself. She had coped admirably.

Very admirably!

'Are you really taking me to the islands? In your speedboat?'

'What? No arguments?'

'Would there be any point?'

'None at all. Did you bring a bikini with you?'

Kate laughed as they crossed the road. 'It isn't that hot yet!' But it would be, she supposed, in a few more weeks. If she were still here. 'Anyhow, I've got a costume with me. One piece.'

'Pity about that.' Adam grinned as they started climbing what Kate later discovered were called the pier steps. It seemed there were hundreds of them, they led up from the sea-front into the High Street, a narrow, quaint little street made from cobblestones.

'Adam, this is gorgeous!' She gasped the words out, breathless from the climb. 'Have we time to look round the shops?'

'This is Sarnia, dear girl. We don't live at a break-neck pace here, we're civilised. Of course there's time.'

'Sarnia? What's that?'

He looked at her in disgust. 'Sarnia means Guernsey. It's the old name for Guernsey. Sarnia, *Sarnia Chérie, gem of the sea*.' he added fondly. 'Don't you know anything about the island, you wretch? How can you have stayed here for weeks and not learnt anything? It's a disgrace!'

Kate's laughter was smug. 'The Channel Islands,' she began, sounding like a tourist guide, 'are the only remaining parts of Normandy still giving allegiance to the English Crown. It's to the English Crown, and not to the British Government, that the Islands' loyalty is directed. Strictly speaking, the Channel Islands own England because in the year 1066, William, Duke of Normandy, became King of England after defeating the English King, Harold, at the Battle of Hastings. England and Normandy were thereby united under a leader who was both the Duke of Normandy and the King of England. The islands are self-governing and are split into two groups, Bailiwicks, so named because the civic head of each group is known as the Bailiff.

Jersey is separate from Guernsey, but Herm and Sark——' She had to break off and catch her breath again.

Adam wouldn't give her best. 'So you've done some homework, eh? Not bad—for a foreigner. Look at you! You're not half as fit as your Aunt Dolly and she's three times your age. You're a disgrace.'

'So you keep telling me.' Kate's chest was heaving. Lord, she really was out of condition. If she carried on like this, she'd be getting fat, too. 'It's all going to change,' she told him firmly. 'I'm going to start a new regime and get healthy again. I don't want to start putting weight on, for heaven's sake.'

'Why ever not? You're tall, you can take it, a stone or so, at any rate.'

'I'm a model, remember?'

Adam stopped walking, turned to look at her.

Their eyes met and held.

Kate was disconcerted. They were standing smack in the middle of the High Street, just looking at each other.

'Well,' he said quietly, 'I'm pleased you're thinking positively at last.'

So was she. 'I—yes, I am. Even if the plastic surgery doesn't do all I'm hoping for, I'll still be able to model. Clothes. My photographic days will still be over, but that doesn't matter.'

He was still looking into her eyes, oddly, she thought. 'And is that what you want, Kate? To model again? To go back to that familiar lifestyle?'

'Of course it is. Naturally.'

'Naturally.' He repeated the word softly, seeming to weigh it. 'Naturally. Mmm. Come on, let's have something to eat before we go any further. I've a few things to pick up here and then we're off to the docks to collect some materials I've had sent over.' He smiled, an easy, friendly smile. 'Then you'll realise why I drive a pick-up truck.'

*   *   *

The following day, Sunday, was the day when Kate's confidence started to return in abundance. She had bought in Town all the make-up she would never have travelled without, prior to the accident. But since the crash she hadn't used any, not only because it was pointless but also because her skin had been in no condition to take it.

On Sunday morning she put all her skills to work and did a superb job. Her violet eyes looked so good, it was difficult to get past them for further scrutiny of her features. She dressed properly, too, in a deep red, figure-hugging dress which had a little hat to match. Black leather shoes, belt and bag completed the outfit and she looked at herself in the full length mirror, nodding in satisfaction.

Adam and Dolores were waiting in the living-room.

'Kate, you look marvellous!' Aunt Dolly was on her feet, hugging her. 'Oh, I'm so pleased, so pleased to see you looking like this!'

Adam, sprawled in an armchair and hidden behind a newspaper, said, 'I take it you girls are ready—finally.' He condescended to put the paper aside and stood up.

It was Kate's turn to be surprised. She had never seen him in a suit before. He was dressed expensively, in a light grey suit with a pale blue silk shirt and a deeper toning tie. He looked gorgeous, there was no denying it. Or did she see him that way merely because this was such a change from his usual garb?

'You look good, Kate,' he said simply, his eyes travelling slowly over her.

'So do you.'

They went in the Volvo to the St Margaret's Lodge Hotel and had a couple of drinks in the bar first, followed by a traditional roast. They all chose the same one, roast beef with Yorkshire pudding. Dolores hardly stopped talking throughout, she seemed as pleased as Punch because Kate had stopped living like a prisoner.

'Ten pounds,' Adam said to Kate later, much later, after Dolly had gone to bed. They were having a nightcap together in the living-room and their conversation had flowed without any arguments at all. 'I believe I owe you ten pounds. I forgot. Should have given it to you earlier.'

Kate was laughing. 'What are you talking about? I make it a fiver!'

'Aha! So you noticed?'

She was still laughing. Yes, she'd noticed the barman in the hotel, he'd hardly been able to take his eyes off her and he hadn't been very subtle about it. 'I'll let you off, Adam. I don't think he counts. He was very young and——'

'Young? He must have been ninety if he were a day!'

'We're obviously not talking about the same person. I'm thinking about the barman.'

'I'm thinking about the old devil who was sitting by the piano with his wife. He stared, all right. At your legs!' He got up and waved a blue ten-pound note under her nose. The colour of notes are the opposite way round in Guernsey. Different from England. Fivers are brown.

Kate shook her head. 'I can't accept that! I thought the bet was only on the supermarket.'

'I didn't say that. Take it, it belongs to you fair and square.'

She took it, highly amused by his insistence. 'You're clearly too principled to welsh on a bet.'

He grunted at that. 'This is the end of that nonsense. No more payouts. I can't afford it!'

'Are you feeling quite well?' she asked cheekily, cocking her head to one side and giving him her most mischievous smile. 'You're flattering me. Again.'

'No, I'm not. I'm simply stating fact. I'm a realist. Good night, Kate. No more nightmares, now.'

She sat in silence after he'd gone, thinking about him.

What a curious man he was, once one got to know him. There were many sides to him and she had the feeling she'd seen only a few. And, oddly enough, he had started to interest her. She felt curiously deflated by his abrupt departure.

Adam's speedboat was moored at Beaucette Marina, at the north of the island. It had vanished from the house a couple of weeks earlier, she'd noticed that but she hadn't thought to ask where it was. Now, as she stepped into it, she felt a rush of excitement. It was a glorious, sunny day. The sky was a deep shade of blue and was cloudless.

Aunt Dolly, unfortunately, wasn't with them. She would have been able to join them had they gone out in the boat the previous day, but the weather had been unkind. It had rained solidly for hours.

'It's going to stay like this for a week, they reckon.' Adam, standing at the wheel, turned to smile at her. 'I got a detailed forecast from the weather men at the airport. So we'll have a bit of fun. I'll take you up in the plane tomorrow. We can pop over to Dinard for lunch.'

Pop over to France? For a meal? It certainly sounded like fun but Kate wasn't up to it. She didn't have the courage. She would have, once, but her sense of adventure seemed to have vanished since the car crash. The idea of going up in a tiny aeroplane did not appeal in the least. On the contrary, it frightened her. She was about to tell Adam this when he switched on the boat's engine and revved it. There was a powerful *brroom*! as he gave it throttle, then he eased up and steered the craft slowly out of the marina.

Kate went to stand by his side, fascinated as they moved on the high tide through the great walls of rock which enclosed the harbour like protective arms, and then they were out on the open sea.

'Hold on,' she was warned. 'We'll go to Sark first. At seventy knots.'

'*Seventy*?' Was he serious?

He was. The speedboat accelerated and accelerated until they were shooting across the channel like an arrow, bouncing off the water and slamming on to it again at full belt. Kate had to yell at him over the noise. Sea spray was all around them, catching their hair, the wind whipping it in all directions. 'I love it! Adam, this is great! I love it, love it, *love* it!'

She loved Herm, too. After a couple of hours' exploration on Sark they headed back to Herm, which is smaller, a tiny dot of an island picture-postcard pretty. They had an alfresco lunch and then walked across the island to the Shell Beach. 'Like Sark, there are no cars on Herm,' Adam told her, 'it's so small, it wouldn't be practical.'

'It certainly wouldn't be desirable, either,' Kate said, falling in love with the place on sight. There was limited accommodation for visitors on the island, those who liked the quietest of holidays, a few houses, a school which was attended by some seven pupils, and like Sark, Herm had a fascinating history. As they walked Adam talked of the days when Herm was used by pirates, of smuggling between France and England, of profiteers and old time adventurers.

It was amazingly hot there considering it was early April.

'I told you.' Adam spread towels on the sand and watched her as she stripped off her slacks and blouse. She was wearing her swimming costume underneath. 'It's very easy to get sunburned on this particular beach, you must watch it, your skin's very pale.'

So it was. But it wouldn't be for long. Kate always got tanned quickly and she lay back revelling in the sunshine. Her eyes closed. She opened them again when Adam stirred, looking up to see him stripping off. It was a glorious sight, he had a magnificent body, tanned, taut, solid. She looked away quickly when he caught her eyes on him. 'I—think I'll have a walk round the beach and do a bit of exploring in the rocks.'

Adam seemed to be stifling a smile, and it annoyed her. What had he seen in her eyes, her appreciation at the sight of him almost naked? She hoped not. 'Watch yourself on the rocks,' he said. 'And don't talk to any strange men.'

'There aren't many around,' she quipped. 'And they look pretty normal to me.'

Twenty minutes later she came back to him, two ice-cream cones in her hands. 'Are you asleep?'

'I was. Thank you very much, you wretched woman!' He opened one eye and peered up at her. 'Would you mind telling me how you paid for those? Have you got a secret pocket in that costume or do you wear a money belt next to your skin?'

Giggling, she thrust her hand at him. 'You'd better take this off me before it starts dripping over you.'

Adam pulled himself into a sitting position and looked up at the sky, shading his eyes against the sun. There was a tiny orange-coloured aircraft flying overhead, one of the Aurigny inter-island planes Kate saw several times a day. She assumed it was on its way to the island of Alderney.

'How many engines do those things have?'

'Some have two, some have three. Why?'

She sat, thinking, licking at her ice-cream. 'Well— about your invitation to go flying with you. I want to, I really do, but I'm afraid I haven't got the nerve.'

'You came to Guernsey by plane.'

'Yes, but it was much bigger than that thing and it had at least two engines! Maybe more, for all I know. I mean, what happens if the one engine fails?' She squinted up at the sky, shivering slightly at her own thoughts.

'They don't. At least, not often!'

'I'm serious, Adam.'

He turned to look at her. 'So you are. Kate, have you any idea how many precautions one takes, checks one makes, before taking an aeroplane up? I got my Private Pilot's Licence when I was eighteen and you can take it from me, the training and testing is very thorough indeed. It isn't like getting a driving licence, you know, one has to have regular medicals to check on fitness, eyesight and so on. As for the maintenance of the aircraft——'

'I appreciate all that, but what happens if the one engine fails?' she persisted.

'Then you glide in.'

'Glide?'

'Of course. And you land where you can, in a field or whatever's handy. You must try it, it's like being in a different world up there. It's like riding on the back of a big bird, the sense of freedom is marvellous.'

She could imagine that. 'But—surely one could only glide for so long? It's probably okay between the islands, but what would you do if you were halfway to France or something and the engine failed?'

'Could be tricky,' he conceded. 'I suppose the answer to that is, one prays.'

'Then that settles it. I'm not going to try it!' She popped the last of the ice-cream in her mouth and lay down.

'Well, well, well,' he said, in that irritating way of his, 'you disappoint me yet again, Kate. You really are a coward.'

'It isn't a question of cowardice,' she said reasonably. 'Why go looking for trouble? Why take risks deliberately?'

'Why do you walk across roads? Why eat in strange restaurants, ride in cars, travel in boats? You can't live your life not doing things just in case something goes wrong. If you're going to worry constantly about being knocked down, poisoned, crunched or drowned or whatever, you might as well wrap yourself up in cotton wool and stick yourself in a cupboard.'

She was about to protest at his exaggeration but his point was fair enough. 'Yes, but to invite disaster when——'

'And I'll tell you something else,' he went on. 'The cupboard and the cotton wool wouldn't be a protection.' Quite suddenly, his expression changed and his eyes seemed to grow darker.

'Adam?' He had turned away, was looking out to sea. 'What is it? What are you thinking about?'

'Nothing.' He didn't turn round. His gravelly voice was barely audible when he added, 'When your number is up, that's it. You go when you're meant to. It doesn't matter where you are, who you are, or what you happen to be doing at the time.'

Kate didn't say anything else. She was looking at the broad expanse of his back, watching in fascination the movement of muscles under the smooth skin. What is he thinking about? she wondered. Or rather, who is he thinking about? The urge to touch him was growing stronger in her with every passing minute. It saddened her, the sudden return of tension between them. In an effort to snap him out of this strange mood she said, 'You're right. I will try it, I will!'

He turned slowly to look at her and when he did so, he seemed to look straight through her. He said, 'Don't do me any favours.'

For Kate the day was ruined. He had not spoken nastily, in fact it seemed as if he were still talking to himself rather than her, but she knew a crushing sense of disappointment.

Blow it, she thought, lying down and closing her eyes. She would sleep for a while, and to hell with him. He had been a thorn in her side for too long and—come to think of it—what had possessed her to come out for an entire day with him?

The next morning, she refused point blank when he announced he was taking her out again. It was at the breakfast table, in the nook in the kitchen. Aunt Dolly was there, bustling about, cooking eggs and bacon and enjoying waiting on the two of them. 'Pour the tea, would you, Kate? I'll have your food ready in a minute.'

'How many sugars in your tea, Adam?'

'None.' He grinned. 'You should know that by now.'

'You normally have coffee.'

'So I do. Now, here's the plan for today. We're going to drive to the north of the island——'

'No.' Kate interrupted him politely but firmly. 'I've got jobs to do.'

'What jobs?' Aunt Dolly spoke up. 'There's nothing that can't wait. Dear me, no! Off you go and enjoy yourselves, take advantage of this lovely weather.'

'Dolores has spoken.' Adam was laughing, seemingly in high spirits today. 'Besides, since when did you get so domesticated?'

'Since ... never mind that.' Kate shifted uneasily. She wasn't exactly *domesticated*! 'I don't intend to spend the whole day working, but there are a few jobs to be done.'

'Let them wait.'

'No, I must——'

'I see.' The amusement had gone from his eyes. 'What you mean is, you don't want to spend another day with me?'

It was a direct challenge. Kate glanced over at her aunt before answering, lowering her voice as she spoke. 'That's the top and bottom of it. Yes.'

'Did you hear that, Mum?' Adam spoke up, ignoring Kate's glare. 'She doesn't want to spend the day with me, she still thinks I'm a swine.'

'Don't be silly, Adam.' Dolores dismissed it completely. 'Kate's never thought any such thing! And please don't swear.'

Kate was silently mouthing to Adam precisely what she did think of him.

'What was that?' he bellowed, laughing again. 'I'm the biggest bastard under the sun?'

'Adam!' His stepmother turned from the cooker to peer at him. 'What's come over you? You know I won't tolerate that kind of language! And I'm quite sure Kate doesn't appreciate it, either.'

Kate bit into her cheeks, having a great deal of trouble suppressing her laughter. Behind her aunt's back she wagged a finger at Adam, her deep blue eyes sparkling like jewels.

'You can take that smug look off your face,' he said, normal voice. 'You're under orders, remember? One way or the other, you're coming out with me for the day. But fear not,' he added, holding up a hand against her protests. 'It's only for a few days more. I'm going to Italy soon so you can do what you want while I'm gone.'

'To Italy?'

'Adam's holding some classes at an art institution in Florence next week,' Aunt Dolly put in, as if he weren't present. 'He'll be back for Easter, when your parents get here. Don't worry.'

'No, don't worry,' Adam added drily. 'Whatever you do, I don't want you to worry, Kate. Will you miss me *terribly* while I'm gone?'

An hour later when they were driving up the west coast of the island, he asked what all that nonsense had been about at breakfast. They were meeting Aunt Dolly in Town for lunch, but that was hours away yet. And in the evening they were having dinner alone in a hotel. Dolores was going out for a long neglected game of bridge with some friends.

Kate turned to him with a look of disdain. 'I can only

stand you in small doses. After a while, you start
irritating me all over again.'

'Is that a fact?'

'Yes. So I'd appreciate it if you'll give me the day off
tomorrow.' It was only when the words were out that
she stopped to think. *How* had he managed to do it?
How had he manipulated her into this? Why had she
been so affected by the unspoken threat he'd issued
over breakfast? She was taking him too seriously! 'And
another thing,' she added, her old assertiveness coming
to the fore, 'I'm not going out to dinner with you
tonight. There's an old film I want to watch on TV, and
even if there weren't, I'd still rather—Adam, what are
you doing?'

He was pulling off the road, that's what he was
doing. He was bringing the car to a halt near a vast,
concrete fortification on the edge of the sea. There were
many such structures around, leftovers from the time
the islands had been occupied by the Germans during
World War II.

'We'd better get a few things sorted out.' He switched
off the engine and turned to her, his face impassive, his
voice brisk. 'You were a pain in the neck to me for
weeks on end. Don't interrupt! Your very presence, the
daily sight of you, was annoying to me. You moved
around like a ghost, you hardly spoke, and when you
deigned to, you were constantly sarcastic.

'Now then, I've discovered you're not as boring as
I thought you were, after all, and until such time as I
tire of you, you will continue to entertain me. And I will
entertain you. By getting you out of the house and
showing you my lovely island.'

'Well, that takes the biscuit!' She laughed at him, not
knowing there was uncertainty in her eyes. 'I've heard
everything now, but I've never heard such arrogance!
I'm more than capable of entertaining myself, thanks
very——'

For such a big man, he moved with remarkable stealth. Before she could finish what she was saying, his arm was around her slender waist and the top of her body was crushed against his chest. His kiss was more like a punishment.

The idea of fighting him off was ridiculous, she didn't even try. Instead she deliberately went rigid and clamped her lips firmly together. This was a punishment, of course it was, for trying to defy him. But who did he think he was, trying to take control of her? All this ran through her mind as she continued to resist him.

'So that's how it is, eh?' Adam lifted his head just long enough to let her see his amusement, then his mouth was on hers once again and her lips were forced apart by the pressure of his. Things changed rapidly, drastically. One minute she was holding herself like steel, the next minute she was melting against him, aware of every inch of contact their bodies were making. She was suddenly unwillingly sensitised to everything, most especially the feel of his mouth on hers. His lips had started to probe rather than punish, his lips and his tongue.

'Adam——' Kate pulled her head back, unnerved, alarmed. What had happened? Why had she started kissing him back?

'What now, Kate? What's worrying that stubborn mind of yours now?'

'I'm——' She could hardly think straight, she was so aware of him, of his nearness, his physical power, his touch. His fingers were brushing her face, moving ever so lightly over her cheekbone, the line of her jaw, in a way she found curiously sensual. 'Stop that, please!' She slapped his hand away. She was no longer conscious of the damage to her face, not with him, but it bothered her very much that his touch was arousing. Worse, when both his hands came back and started all over again, the resistance went out of her. She was looking at him, enjoying what he was doing, trying to fathom what was in his eyes.

'You can't blame me for kissing you, for wanting to touch you,' he was saying. 'You're beautiful. You have such marvellous bones, do you know that?'

With any other man, she would have laughed at that. With him, she couldn't. There was a detachedness about him now, she realised that the sculptor in him was very serious about what he was saying. No wonder his touch was affecting her so, his fingers were loving what they were doing. They were moving inch by inch over her face, over her brows, her nose, her lips. Then they were under her chin, her head was tilted back a little and he was kissing her again.

She moaned softly against his mouth before parting her lips willingly to invite his exploration. Every inch of her body was responding now and she pressed herself closer, enjoying the feel of his chest against the softness of her breasts.

When they finally drove off, Adam seemed unmoved by the experience but Kate was shaken to the core. Dear Lord, what was she going to discover about him next? Never, ever, had she experienced such sensuality in a man, such unexpected tenderness after something very close to violence.

What had they been talking about to begin with? She couldn't even remember. Fascinated, she turned to study his profile as they drove; he was singing now, singing softly to himself as if nothing had happened, as if he hadn't a care in the world!

'Adam?'

'Yes, Kate?'

'I—please don't do that again. I don't want——'

'You're disappointing me again. Please don't lie to me. I can tolerate many faults and foibles in women but I can't stand silly lies. Okay? I shall kiss you whenever the fancy takes me and you will enjoy it as much as you enjoyed it just now.'

Kate turned to look out of the window, saying nothing. No, she wouldn't lie, but she wasn't going to admit he was right, either! Something had gone terribly wrong somewhere along the line. In the past, with other men she had dated, it had been she who played the games, she who called the shots, she who was in control. If she were honest, she had hitherto been unimpressed, unmoved by every single man she'd been out with, finding serious faults sooner or later, usually sooner, with them all.

But she respected Adam de la Mare in many ways, though she'd die rather than let him know it. The physical attraction she felt for him was new to her and the extent of it shocked her. Moreover, while she was being honest with herself she might as well admit that she'd felt it to some extent from the moment she'd set eyes on him.

Turning to steal another rapid look at him, she thought it a pity she didn't like him as a person.

CHAPTER SIX

'Who is Elena?'

'Elena? Oh! Do you mean Adam's friend?'

'Er—well, that's what I was wondering. Is she a girlfriend of his? She's Italian, I take it?' Kate was making a potato salad, she had her back to her aunt and was keeping her voice casual.

It was Good Friday morning and her parents were coming on the lunch-time flight. She and Dolores were preparing a meal before going to meet them at the airport.

Adam wasn't back yet. He had taken a commercial flight to Italy and was supposed to have come home last night. Instead, during the afternoon, there had been a phone call from him. Kate had taken it. 'Is anything wrong? Where are you?'

'No, no, nothing's wrong. I've been delayed, that's all. I'll be back on Guernsey some time tomorrow with luck, Saturday at the latest. I'm at home at the moment.'

And there had been music playing in the background. She couldn't help wondering whether he'd been alone.

Kate's curiosity, her concern, had amazed her. It shouldn't have, because she had missed Adam while he'd been gone. For the first time ever, she had been bored these past few days, hardly knowing what to do with herself. Aunt Dolly had been out as often as usual, Kate had been restless. Time and again she had caught herself looking in the direction of his empty studio. It was perverse of her, she knew that. She should have been glad of the peace Adam's absence represented. Worse, since taking the call from him the previous afternoon, she'd been wondering why he had been 'delayed'. What could he be doing on Good Friday in Italy? Not teaching, that was for sure.

'Yes, she's Italian,' Aunt Dolly was saying. 'And I suppose you could call her a girlfriend. She and Adam are more than just friends, if that's what you mean. He's known her for a couple of years. She's an art restorer, a very gifted girl. She works in Florence and lives in Siena, not too far from Adam's home.'

'Is she . . . I was wondering . . .' Kate stopped herself. She wanted to know more but she didn't want to appear too interested. This was crazy, really. She didn't want to *be* interested at all!

But she'd given her aunt a good reason to natter, and natter she did. 'Oh, Elena's a lovely girl! Well, she's about thirty, I suppose. She's been married and has one daughter. I met them both when I was visiting Adam a couple of years ago. He hadn't known her long then. She and her little girl came over here for a week last year and I was surprised the relationship had lasted that long. I dared to hope . . . but I don't know what the situation is with them now. I don't think Adam will ever marry.'

'Why not?' Unthinking, Kate turned round to look curiously at her aunt. But she found herself looking at her back; Dolly was standing at the sink, washing lettuces. 'Because of Margaret, of course. I don't think anyone will ever replace her in Adam's affections.'

'Margaret?'

Dolores turned round then. 'Margaret Mahy, his fiancée.'

'*Fiancée?* But I—I don't know anything about this. My mother never mentioned Adam was engaged.'

'For three years.' Aunt Dolly looked troubled. 'There's no reason Anne should have mentioned it to you. Margaret died fifteen years ago, when you were about six. She's long gone but she's not forgotten. Take

my advice, Kate, don't mention her to Adam, ever.
He'll fly off the handle.'

It was a moment before Kate could gather her wits.
'No, I—I won't.' She had seen Adam in a temper more
often than she cared to, a temper she had provoked,
usually unwittingly. There was no way she would
deliberately anger him! 'What happened to her? How
long had he known her? He must have been very young
when he met her?'

'He was your age when Margaret died, twenty-one.
She was a Guernsey girl, the same age. They'd known
one another since they were fifteen and they became
inseparable—until Adam left for Guildford, for the art
school. They got engaged before he left and he came
home as often as he could. Margaret trained as a nurse,
here on the island, and then she went to St
Bartholomew's in London for further training and
experience. By then Adam was at the Royal Academy
and they were planning their wedding. Put the kettle on,
Kate, will you? We've time for a cuppa before we leave
for the airport.'

It was ten minutes before Kate got the rest of the
story. She had to wait until the tea was made and they
sat down to drink it. Everything was ready for her
parents' arrival. 'So how did Margaret die, Aunt Dolly?
Did she take ill?'

'Oh, no, no. She was as healthy as can be, a beautiful
girl. I was very, very fond of her. No, she died in a train
crash. A derailment, rather. You won't remember it but
it was all over the papers at the time. The train was
going from London to Glasgow. Margaret was on her
way to a lecture or a convention or something. It was
something to do with her career, anyhow. Forty-two
people were killed and . . . she was one of them.'

Silence.

Dolores went into her own thoughts for a moment, as
did Kate. So that's what Adam had been thinking

about, that day on the beach on Herm, when she'd
protested about taking risks. No wonder he thought so
philosophically. 'It doesn't matter who you are,' he'd
said, 'or what you are, when your number's up, that's
it.'

It didn't matter how old you were, either. How
horrible. Poor Margaret! Twenty-one years old and . . .
'Adam took it very hard, I suppose?'

'Hard?' Dolores closed her eyes and shuddered. 'He
didn't do a thing for six months. He came home and he
stayed home. Here, I mean, he didn't have his house in
Tuscany then. Roland and I despaired of his ever
returning to normal. He didn't do a thing, not a thing,
for six months. It was a dreadful time and I hope he
never has to endure anything like that again.' Dolores
pushed her cup aside and stood up. 'He's known plenty
of women since, of course, but none of them have
lasted—except Elena. Still, I don't know how things
stand between them now, as I say. I think there's
something to be gathered from the fact that she isn't
coming to Guernsey this year. Perhaps the relationship
is on the wane.'

And there again, perhaps it wasn't. Adam was with
her right now, wasn't he?

He came back mid-afternoon on Saturday. Dolores,
Kate and her parents had been out for lunch and were
drinking tea and sunning themselves in the garden when
Adam appeared. He had left his pick-up at the airport
on leaving and he hadn't phoned to announce his
return.

'Good afternoon, all!' The first warning Kate had
was the sound of his voice. She was sitting with her
back to the house and hadn't seen him approach.
'Anne, George, it's good to see you. Sorry I wasn't back
for your arrival, had business to see to in Italy. How are
you both?'

'We're fine, fine!' Kate's father shook him heartily by

the hand, slapped him on the shoulder. Anne turned her face up for a kiss and Dolly went into the house for an extra teacup.

Then he gave Kate a nod. 'And how's Kate?'

'I'm——'

'Look at her!' Anne Sumner had hardly stopped fussing over her daughter since stepping off the plane. 'She's looking so well, I can't tell you how pleased I am! Why she's almost her old self again, and I believe we have you to thank for this, Adam.'

'Me?' He eased his huge frame on to the grass, sitting cross-legged and laughing. 'I'm not sure what you mean, Anne.'

Kate wanted to speak up but to her dismay she found herself tongue-tied, something her 'old self' would never have been. But then she was and was not the girl she used to be. Right now, she was experiencing sheer pleasure at the sight of Adam de la Mare, to the extent that her breathing had gone suddenly awry. She had felt such—such a shock on seeing him. It had occurred to her over the past few days that what she felt for Adam now was gratitude. Having done a lot of thinking about him, about their strange relationship and the way it had changed, she had realised just how much he had been responsible for bringing her back to normal. It still held true that she didn't like his methods but—well, they had worked. As she looked at him now, though, she knew it was more than gratitude she felt towards him. Or was it was something quite different? Something as well as, perhaps? Or instead of?

He turned to her, grinning. 'What does your mother mean, Kate? And why are you looking at me as if I've grown an extra head while I've been away?'

She managed to laugh but it sounded strained. 'An extra pair of horns, more like. I've told Mum and Dad how you bullied me into getting out of that armchair I was glued to.'

'Bullied you? Dearest Kate, it isn't in my nature to bully anyone, least of all a frail young thing such as you!' He turned back to her parents. 'I merely suggested it would be better for Kate to take a walk now and then, get some colour into her cheeks.'

Anne was peering at her daughter again, serious now. 'I can't get over how good her face looks, the way she's healed. Nature is wonderful.'

'Mum, would you mind not talking about me as if I'm not here?' Kate laughed again and forced herself to look at her parents, not to keep feasting her eyes on Adam. 'Dad, you haven't given me my post yet, I thought you were calling into my flat to collect it for me? Wasn't there any?'

'Oh, I forgot to give it to you!' George gave her an apologetic look. Kate had sent him a spare key to her flat and had asked him to call in when next he was in London. He went there almost every week. 'There's a stack of it, it's upstairs. We were so busy talking last night——'

'I can imagine,' Adam put in. 'Dolly was giving you an update, right?'

'Right!' George Sumner put a match to his pipe, looking heavenward, 'If there's one thing your mother's good at, it's talking!'

'I heard that.' Dolores was back. 'It's because I live on my own most of the year. People get like that, you know.'

'I wasn't complaining,' her nephew said hastily, sincerely. 'By the way, Kate, it looks as if your rent's overdue. There are two envelopes from your landlord's agents.'

'I know, I'll send them a cheque straight away.'

'And what about Roger?' Anne asked. 'He's phoned us several times, as you know. Have you let him know where you are yet?'

'Who's Roger?' This, from Adam.

'Roger Dennison, an admirer,' Anne answered.

'One of the many,' George put in. 'You wouldn't believe how many bouquets of flowers were sent to us when Kate left the nursing home in London. She hadn't told her friends she was coming here, so they assumed she'd come home to us. They didn't phone to ask, they just sent the flowers. Stacks of them! When people did start to phone—well, Roger mainly, we had to tell them Kate wasn't with us. I think it was unfair of you really,' he said to his daughter, 'not to let us tell people where you were, are.'

'That's how I wanted it, Dad. And it still stands, don't tell anyone.'

'When are you going home, love?'

'When it's time to see the specialist in London.'

Adam was looking interested, if somewhat puzzled. But he said nothing, asked no more questions.

Easter was fun, there was only one cloudy afternoon throughout the holidays and every hour was made good use of. They all went over to Herm, they ate out often, Adam took Kate's parents for a spin in his plane, at which point Kate stayed at home with Dolores. He also took next door's children up, William and John; not, it seemed, for the first time. And on the Sumners' last day, they had a meal with the boys' parents, at their home. Kate had got to know them all quite well by then, she'd spent many an hour over tea with Catherine and Jim Sarre.

Fun though it was, Kate was glad when her parents went home and things returned to normal. The thought, the feeling, struck her as odd. Normal? She didn't belong on Guernsey, didn't belong with Dolores and Adam. But it felt as though she did. On the night of her parents' departure, she and Adam had their first hour alone after Dolores had gone to bed.

'So,' he said, after switching off the TV after the ten o'clock news. The news was almost all he ever watched on the television, that and the odd documentary or concert. 'Why all the secrecy? Why did you tell your parents not to let your friends know where you are?'

'Because I quickly discovered there's nobody I can really call a friend. As far as the females are concerned, they're mostly other models and I think they saw my near-destruction as one less piece of competition.'

'That's a very callous thing to say! It doesn't sound as if you gave them much chance to demonstrate their friendship.'

Kate shrugged. 'It's true I wouldn't allow any visitors other than family, but my friends' letters and messages to the hospital all seemed to be shrouded with embarrassment. That's how it struck me at the time and I still think I'm right. People didn't quite know what to say to me. Real friends would have.'

Adam shook his head. 'I think you're being too hard on them. Anyhow, what about Roger?'

'Ha! He was supposedly in love with me. He came to the hospital but he accepted the situation lamely when I refused to see him.'

'It doesn't sound as if you're in love with him.' Adam was sitting on the floor, his long legs stretched before him, his back resting against the settee. Kate was about three feet away, in her favourite chair, with her legs curled under her, her arms folded and a cynical look on her face.

'Got it in one,' she said. 'I've never been in love in my life.'

'How very sad. Give it time. You're just a girl.'

'Don't patronise me, Adam. I'm twenty-one years old.'

He laughed at that. 'All right, you're past it. Too old, hard and cynical to be susceptible to that most wondrous and sometimes monstrous of emotions.'

'Now who's been cynical?'

'I'm entitled. Unlike you.'

It was on the tip of her tongue to say, 'Because of what happened to Margaret?' but she dared not. She said nothing.

'I'm off to bed.' Adam surprised her by getting up. He stood in the middle of the room, stretching.

Kate couldn't take her eyes off him. She thought of his remark, 'I'm just a great big pussy cat.' What a joke! Panther, more like. 'I—was just about to make some coffee.'

'Not for me, thanks.'

She was disappointed. 'It's not like you to turn in so early.' This was true but she wished she hadn't said it. She didn't want him to guess her disappointment.

Adam made no comment. He came over to her, caught hold of her hand and pulled her to her feet. 'Good night, Kate.'

She knew what he was about to do and, against her better judgment, she co-operated fully. They kissed, as if it were the most natural thing to do. And yet, again, she wished she hadn't shown willing. Adam was a mystery to her and she had not forgotten his peculiar treatment of her the day before he'd left for Italy.

After several days of sight-seeing and exploring with him, days when they had talked jokingly and often very seriously about all sorts of things, days when they had, she thought, become friends, he had quite suddenly turned cold on her. On the day before he left, he had told her to come for him at nine o'clock, and she remembered vividly walking into his studio on what should have been their last day together—to find him entertaining the two youngsters from next door.

'Well, what's going on here?' Kate had laughed on seeing both boys with plaster on their right hands. Adam was, at their request, making a cast for them. The boys thought it great fun.

But she and Adam were supposed to be going out. 'I'm ready whenever you are,' she'd told him. 'Are we leaving after breakfast? You can come and join us for bacon and eggs, boys.'

The children had already had breakfast, they told her, but would come up to the house for some toast.

'I don't want anything.' This, somewhat brusquely, was Adam's answer. 'I'm cancelling today, Kate, you can have your freedom. I have to get on with some work.'

She hadn't known what to say. It was a complete about-face, to her way of thinking. She didn't want her 'freedom'. Had she said or done something to offend him? 'I—yes, of course, if that's what you want, but—is something wrong?'

'Nope. I'm busy.'

Busy, playing with the children? Busy, all of a sudden? 'Er—well, I've got plenty to do,' she answered cheerfully. 'Send the boys up when they've got that plaster off their hands.' She had walked slowly back to the house, disappointed, and cross with herself for feeling like that.

And now he was kissing her hungrily. Just as she was kissing him. When he finally let go of her, pushing his fingers into her hair and smiling into her eyes, he said, 'It seems as though you missed me while I was away.'

'Like a hole in the head.'

She wanted to know whether he'd missed her, she wanted dearly to know how many nights he had spent with Elena. If any. But she couldn't ask either question. At least, not directly. 'So—how were things in Italy? You haven't said.'

'Very pleasant—except for the interview.'

'Interview?'

'With an arts magazine.'

'I take it you don't like being interviewed.'

'I hate it, journalists are not my favourite people. I regard it as an infringement of my privacy—but it's necessary. If the world's going to know about my work, it has to get to see it. Nor do I like posing for photographs.' He broke off, kissing her on the forehead, on her brows. 'Unlike you. But the camera loves you, doesn't it, Kate? I've never known anyone as photogenic.'

'And what would you know about my photographs?'

'I've been looking through your scrapbook. I mean, Dolly's scrapbook.'

'Of *me*?' Kate laughed at the idea. She knew there existed one of Adam but—'I had no idea about this! I haven't seen it around.'

'No.' He smiled, kissing her lightly, swiftly, on the mouth. 'That's because it's in my room at the moment.'

'Oh!' She hardly knew what to say. So he was still studying her bone structure—or something? 'I was wondering—are we going out somewhere tomorrow?'

'We certainly are! Just the two of us. You and I,' he smiled, 'are going flying. Have you got your passport with you?'

'No. I mean yes, I have now.'

'No, yes, now?' He was laughing at her, still holding her close. They were standing and she could feel the length of his body against hers. It was no wonder she couldn't think straight.

'I asked my father to pick it up when he called at my flat. Just in case . . .'

'Good for you. We'll spend the day in France then.' And with that he kissed her again, his arms locking tightly around her as he pulled her even closer.

'Adam . . .' Small gasps of pleasure were issuing from her, making speech almost impossible as his mouth moved over her face, down to the hollow of her neck, up to that sensitive spot behind her ears. Her head was swimming and she was trembling against him. 'I—it seems you've missed me, too.'

'I've missed this,' he spoke against her mouth, teasing her lips with his. 'And, much as I like your

parents, I'm glad they've gone. We haven't had a
moment alone while they've been here.'

She was only too aware of that. 'Adam!' Her
trembling increased as his hands slipped beneath the
flimsy material of her blouse, moving sensuously over
her back then coming round slowly, slowly, to cup her
breasts. She moved away. She wanted him, and she
didn't want to want him. Mad though it seemed, she
still wasn't sure whether she really liked him as a
person, she honestly wasn't sure about that. She
certainly wasn't sure what he thought of her, where she
stood with him.

Nor did she find out when she moved away from his
embrace. 'I—think that's enough.'

Adam's smile was a mixture of scepticism and
genuine amusement. 'Do you, Kate? Do you really?' He
caught hold of her again, his right arm circled her back
and he pulled her hard up against his chest. With his
left hand he caught hold of her chin, holding her face
up to his. His brown eyes were glittering, looking
straight into her mind, or so it seemed. 'It isn't nearly
enough, Kate. You want me, but don't worry, I shan't
let it go to my head.'

Kate stiffened, his smile wasn't altogether pleasant
and ripples of alarm ran through her. Why, she couldn't
say, but she knew a vague feeling of ... fear? A
nameless fear.

'And I want you,' he went on. 'But you mustn't let it
go to your head, either. Good night, Kate.'

Long after he had left the room, she was still
trembling, still aroused, still puzzled by his words and
by his behaviour. She dropped her head into her hands,
very near to tears. Again. Again he was making her cry,
but for very different reasons now. He was confusing
her as much as he was intriguing her. It was another
new experience for her, no man had come close to
doing this before. What *was* it about him? What—why

had she started to weigh and take seriously every
syllable he uttered? And what had his last few words
meant, exactly?

'Do I have to wear that thing?'

''Fraid so.'

They were standing by Adam's plane on a field of
private aircraft belonging to members of the aero club.
Kate had already asked a dozen questions, like,
'Where's the fuel tank?' 'Have you done much gliding,
then?' 'I suppose you had to be trained how to do it?'
'Has the engine ever stalled on you?' And so on.

Adam had answered them all satisfactorily and
patiently but she was still as nervous as a kitten. She
was also excited. What she was complaining about now
was the life-belt thing Adam was strapping her into. She
felt idiotic in it. The straps went right round the body,
crossed at the back, came round the front—and it
wasn't very elegant, to say the least. Nor was it
confidence-inspiring. Did he expect them to take a dip
in the sea before they reached Dinard? If they reached
Dinard . . .

'Is it really necessary to put me in this? I mean, is it
the law or something?'

'It's Adam's law. Now shut up and keep still.'

Adam's law! Oh, well, there was probably no point in
arguing, in that case! Kate looked up at the wings of the
plane and kept still while he finished tying her straps. It
had never occurred to her that the fuel was stored in the
wings. They didn't seem like very big wings. She
supposed they were big enough. It was a small
aeroplane and it got smaller the longer she looked at it.
It wasn't much taller than she was. 'Oh, God!'

'What now?' He was laughing at her again, putting
on his own life belt now, and suddenly she felt better.
Adam knew what he was doing, he always knew what
he was doing. Aunt Dolly had assured her of this earlier

in the morning, several times, but it was something
Kate knew at heart. She only wished she understood
more about the *way* his mind worked.

'Nothing.'

'You're not getting hysterical, are you?'

'Don't be so rude! I'm always in control of myself.'

He gave her an old-fashioned look and proceeded to
tell her what to do with the life jacket in the case of an
emergency—and how to do it. Kate didn't hear a word
of it except for the mention of a whistle, which made
her want to burst out laughing. She bit her cheeks and
nodded wisely, as if understanding everything. In her
mind, there simply could not be, must not be, an
'emergency'. She climbed into the Cessna with very
wobbly legs, only to be battened down with more straps
in the form of a safety belt.

Oh, God! She said it to herself this time.

Then there was a reassuring smile from Adam, a
swift kiss on the cheek, the faint crackle of the radio as
he spoke to Air Traffic Control with his call sign: 'Golf-
Oscar-Foxtrot-Charlie-Mike . . .'

He was given permission to taxi to the runway, the
number of which Kate heard and instantly forgot in her
anxiety. 'Keep your feet away from the pedals,' she was
told.

What pedals? Did one *pedal* the thing to the runway?
Wasn't that rather—primitive? She didn't dare utter a
word, first, because Adam was still communicating by
radio and second because she didn't want to show any
more anxiety. Third, her mouth had gone dry!

They reached the edge of the runway. They took up
their position. Kate watched, her hands clenched on her
lap, as an Air UK flight took off, then a little Aurigny
plane. And then it was their turn! Clearance for take-off
was given . . .

'Pity about that. Did you hear?' Adam was as cool as
could be and so obviously enjoying himself—except for,

'We have to stay at a thousand feet till we speak to Control at Jersey. Kate? Are you all right? Cheer up, we'll be off the ground in a minute!'

Oh, God! Please look after us today, *please*!

A thousand feet? That didn't sound very high! It would be a long way down, though, if . . . It didn't bear thinking about.

They were off the ground, climbing, climbing! Kate looked down at the rapidly diminishing size of the airport. Within minutes Adam was banking, turning south, climbing a little more into the clear blue sky and then—and then the fun began!

Exhilarating was hardly the word for it. It was thrilling, marvellous, the way the little plane obeyed and zoomed its way across the island and over the sea. It was as steady as a rock now, flying straight, and Kate, at last, began to relax.

'How are you doing, beautiful girl?'

'I—it's—oh!'

'That's just how I feel. Have you changed your mind now?'

'Changed my mind?' She was looking down at the white horses on the sea. 'I want to learn how to fly myself!'

'You'd have more success in a plane.'

Kate laughed too loudly and too long, the way one does when nervousness is suddenly dispelled. 'How far is it to Jersey?'

'About fifteen minutes.'

Air Traffic Control at Jersey gave them permission to ascend to four thousand feet. As they left that island's airspace, the voice came over the radio: 'Change to 120.15 for Dinard control.'

'How long before we get to Dinard?'

'From here? About twenty minutes. The wind's with us.' Adam tuned his radio to the Dinard frequency and reported in. The instruction came back to report again when he passed over Cezembre, an island three miles off the coast of France.

'Golf-Oscar-Foxtrot ... re-tune to 120.25 for the control tower.'

There was more to the business of flying than Kate expected. Not only did the instruments look complex (the only ones she recognised were the altimeter and the air speed indicator) but there were all sorts of formalities to see to. Flight plans to file. Weather conditions to be checked on. Airport landing fees to pay. Not that these things took long.

They had lunch in Dinard's small airport restaurant, where Kate made friends with a parrot who didn't say anything, either in English or in French. After that, they took off again—for Cherbourg!

Kate was captive, like the parrot in the cage in the restaurant, and Adam was going to make sure she got over her nervousness once and for all, it seemed.

'Cherbourg? You never mentioned we were going on to Cherbourg! It's miles from Dinard!'

'We'll just have a look round, from the air. Or we can land and I'll buy you a drink, if you like.'

She turned to him, looking very sheepish. 'Adam ... I need to go to the loo.'

'There aren't any up here, beautiful.' He roared with laughter. 'What's up—got your nerves back? Well, hold on, there's a good girl. It won't take long, we're already ten minutes out of Dinard. And that settles it, we'll land, find a loo for you and a bar—in that order! Now then,' he added, serious again, 'keep a look out for aircraft while I consult my maps.'

She thought he was joking. He wasn't. 'No, no, I mean it, keep your eyes skinned, we're out of controlled airspace for the moment.'

Oh, God.

She assumed 'George' was flying the craft now. She hoped so, because Adam wasn't touching any of the controls—he was concentrating on the maps which he opened on his lap. Kate kept looking from him to the sky in front of her, wondering what on earth would happen if she did spot another plane. She spotted one.

'Adam! There's one!'

He looked up, looked at her and turned back to the maps. 'Kate darling, that thing's about six light years away and several million miles above us! Come to think of it, it could be an angel on a cloud.'

She shot him a look of disgust, which he didn't see. What an exaggeration! Humph! She looked down, there was a bit of cloud over France, little wisps of it floating by, under them. She could see a railway quite plainly, through the clear patches.

When they landed at Cherbourg, Adam took her into his arms, beaming at her. 'You're a brave girl, I'm going to reward you!' He pressed a catch which released her seat belt and pulled her closer, bringing his mouth down on hers.

'Adam, let go of me!'

'Now, Kate, I've told you I'm going to kiss you whenever——'

'It's not that, I don't mind that. I mean—well, not too much!' She couldn't help laughing. 'But I've got to get to the loo, I'm bursting!'

'So am I,' he grinned, 'absolutely desperate. For this . . .' He kept her busy for minutes before letting her out. She ran across the tarmac.

Later, hours later, Adam put the Cessna 'to bed' by locking up and putting huge circular blocks of cement in front of its wheels.

'Is that necessary? Is it likely to blow away?'

'Well, it won't now, will it?' he grinned. 'Still want to learn to fly?'

'No.' She took the hand he held out as they walked across the field in the fading light. 'It's far too complicated! But I'll be your passenger any time you want company.' And she meant it.

'Good girl! Come on, we'll have a drink in the club. Or would you rather go home?'

Kate chose to go home. She couldn't wait to tell Aunt Dolly all about her trip—and her courage!

They went swimming the next day. Aunt Dolly went down with them to Moulin Huet Bay and Kate and Adam braved the water. It was the fourth week of April and the sun was quite hot. The water was cold! It was a pretty little bay, rocky but interesting, and there were nice little patches one could swim in. Aunt Dolly didn't move from the shelter of the beach until it was time for lunch. 'Shall we go to the Moulin Huet Hotel, Adam? I didn't book but we'll probably be okay for a table at this time of year. You'll love the views from up there, Kate. From the lounge of the hotel you can see right across the bay.'

'We'll go anywhere you like.'

Anywhere you like. These words were used often in the weeks ahead, when decisions were being made as to where to go, what to do. When the weather was unkind Adam sometimes worked for a few hours. Kate sat in the studio, watching him work, fascinated, finding that she was content just to be with him.

When he wasn't working, he took her sight-seeing in the truck. It was not the most prestigious way to travel but she'd got used to the vehicle by now and she drove as often as not. When Dolores was able to join them they would go flying, circuiting the islands, or they would all go out in the car and Adam would complain at frequent intervals about his stepmother's driving.

They were days of laughter, of interest, of long conversations; days of strolling the beach and exploring and, more often than not, they were days of sunshine.

They couldn't last for ever.

One Monday lunch-time Kate went down to the studio in search of Adam and found him brooding, doing nothing, staring at the view from the huge, north-facing window. 'Adam? Is something wrong? Lunch is ready, you said you'd come up to the house by twelve.'

She glanced round the studio. He had told her he had to make a start on something but the work in progress didn't look much different from the last time she'd been in here. Of course, he'd spent so much time with her, taking her out these past weeks, he hadn't got on with much.

He hadn't heard her speak to him, he wasn't aware she was watching him from the other side of the room. 'Adam? Are you all right?'

Turning swiftly, his brows came together in a scowl. 'What's the matter, Kate? Why are you creeping around?'

The words, his tone, hurt. 'I wasn't. You said ...' Haltingly, she repeated what she'd just said.

Adam grunted, looking away from her. 'What have you done—is it hot or cold?'

'Cold. It's chicken salad.'

'I'll have it in here.'

Kate didn't know what to make of him. Again. Why did he go off like this? After so many happy, carefree days—what had got into him all of a sudden? *Again.*

Feeling miserable, she ventured closer. 'I'll bring it down on a tray for you, all right?'

'Thanks.'

'Is—is there something on your mind?'

He turned to look at her then, straight at her. And yet she had the feeling once more that he wasn't really seeing her. 'Plenty.' He picked up a pencil from his drawing board, started tapping it against his teeth. 'It's nothing for you to be concerned about Kate.' He spoke more gently now, much to her relief. 'I have to get down to some work, real work. Alone.'

It was fair enough. Her eyes moved to a shape on a pedestal, a shape covered with a wet cloth. It looked like a bust. 'Is that—is that a bust of me you've started?'

'Why do you ask?'

'I just wondered. You said——' She shook herself. This wasn't the way she wanted to conduct herself but she was feeling so distanced from him, it hurt more and more with every passing minute. Damn the man, she thought, why don't I just walk away and leave him to it? Why pander to these odd moods of his? You're a fool, Kate. Fancy offering to bring his lunch. Let him fetch it himself!

But what she said was very different from what she was thinking. 'You said you wanted to do a bust of me and—well, I will model for you, if you like.'

'I said at a later date I'd like to do a life-size sculpture.'

She caught the challenge in his eyes, she couldn't fail to. Nude, that's what he meant. Of course, it would mean nothing to him, having a nude model. Old hat, that sort of thing, to him. But—but she'd never modelled nude and while Adam would be totally professional about it, she herself . . . That's all the time it took for things to get worse. While Kate was pausing for thought, Adam's expression turned to one of anger.

'Forget it. In any case, I've changed my mind. I don't want to sculpt you at all, in any size, shape or form.'

'I see. Well, that's all right.' How she managed to keep her voice light, cheerful, she didn't know. His words had hurt her and puzzled her further. Again she wondered what on earth she'd done to upset him. Again she was furious with herself for allowing him to get to her like this.

But what could she do?

That was the power he had over her, over her emotions.

'Kate, wait a minute. Please.'

She had almost got to the door, holding her head high, outwardly composed, when he called her back.

'Look, I'm sorry if I seem—a bit off today. It's just that that,' he jerked a thumb in the direction of the shrouded bust, 'is something I must get on with. It's a special commission for Sir Charles Brouard.'

The name meant nothing to Kate, except that Brouard was a typical Guernsey surname.

'And I'm going to be concentrating on it from now on. Sir Charles will be coming to sit for me and his free time is limited. Okay?'

Irritation got the better of her. She was glad of it. It wasn't like her to be as meek as she had been and she despised herself for it. 'Look, Adam, you don't have to explain anything to me. We've had a super time together and I'm grateful to you. For many things. Of course you have to get on with your work, I know that. And so do I, for that matter. I'm leaving next week.' She added this without thought. It was a spur of the moment decision. But it was the middle of May, after all, and she had been here for three months . . .

Three months?

What was she *thinking* about? Why had she stayed so long? She had to get herself, and her life, together again. She had to get back into the old routine, back to normal. Back to normal in every way, she hoped. Before she could do anything at all, she had to go and talk to the doctor in Harley Street.

She sighed, aloud. Adam had made no comment. 'Anyhow, what I'm saying is we all do our own thing in this house, we come and go as we please, okay?'

It worked. She was rewarded with a smile.

As she hurried across the field, back to the house, her irritation turned rapidly to anger. Anger with herself as much as with him. She had managed to sound nonchalant, thank goodness, but she was inwardly seething. Let him come and get his own lunch, she wasn't going to wait on him!

By the time she reached the kitchen, she was crying.

She dashed up to her room, wanting to be out of the way if he did venture into the house. Damn him, damn him! Right from the start it had been easy for him to hurt her. Wasn't it time she got over it, became immune to it? Things were so different between them these days but . . . but he could still hurt her when he chose to.

No, that wasn't fair. Surely he wasn't doing it deliberately, not now? He was entitled to have moods, like anyone else. Perhaps more so, maybe it was something to do with artistic temperament. And maybe he was feeling pressured because he had neglected his work. For her. Perhaps she should be flattered that he had?

Kate's emotions were see-sawing again, one minute she was finding excuses for him and the next minute she was furious with him. The result was that she paced the floor of her room like an idiot, up and down, up and down. She had to go, get away from him, she had to get back to London.

Yes, she would leave next week. Definitely. She'd have picked up the phone and booked a ticket there and then, except that she must talk to her aunt first. Courtesy demanded that of her. She couldn't just announce her departure abruptly. Aunt Dolly deserved better than that.

But—but she didn't really want to leave.

Damn it all, she didn't want to leave Guernsey. Not as long as Adam was here. When she thought of the number of times he had taken her in his arms of late, when she thought how much she wanted him physically, she almost screamed. Thank goodness she had drawn the line with him. Last week, in the early hours of the morning, after endless cups of coffee and an exchange of views, a long talk about—she couldn't even remember now—they had started kissing. The difference was that on that occasion, Adam had shown none of his usual restraint.

He had forgotten, or so it seemed, where they were. In the living-room of Dolly's house. With no guaranteed privacy. It had been Kate who called a halt, Kate who remembered who they were and where they were—eventually.

All the more reason to get away as quickly as possible, she told herself now. If she stayed here much longer, she would end up making love with Adam. There was no doubt about that.

Dolores was not home twenty-four hours a day.

CHAPTER SEVEN

'DID you get your flight confirmation, Kate?'

'Yes, they phoned this morning and said they'd had a cancellation. I'm leaving on Sunday, after breakfast.'

'So did you ring the surgeon? Did you get an appointment with him?'

'Yes. For next Thursday. Come and put your feet up, Aunt Dolly, you look a bit tired. The kettle's boiled, I'll make us some tea.'

It was Friday, a little after four. Aunt Dolly had just got in. Kate had spent most of the day walking the dogs and sitting on the beach. That was virtually all she'd done for the past five days. 'I was lucky to get such an early appointment, I suppose that's one of the advantages of going privately,' she called from the kitchen.

She'd been lucky to get a flight, too. She hadn't realised how much in demand aeroplane seats were once the holiday season was under way; she'd had to wait, hope, for a cancellation. Given her choice, she'd have flown away from Guernsey last Monday, after that difficult scene in Adam's studio. But she had had to talk to her aunt.

Dolores had been very understanding; she knew as well as everyone else that Kate had to resume her life some time or another.

'Are you all right, Aunt Dolly?' Kate came in with the tea tray and caught the worried expression on her aunt's face. 'Are you tired?'

'Me? Since when?' She was smiling now. 'I'll pour, dear. No, I'm just—to tell you the truth, I'm going to miss you. I love having you here, Kate. It's so nice to

112

have young people around, especially my favourite niece.'

Kate hugged her. It wasn't really like Dolly to wax sentimental; she was touched. 'And I've loved being here. I don't know how to thank you for your kindness. You've been wonderful to me.'

'Hush, now! You're better, what more could I want? Why don't you fetch another cup and take Adam some tea? Has he emerged from his studio at all today?'

'Once, to my knowledge.'

'He seems—not quite himself at the moment. Don't you think so?'

Kate couldn't be sure what Adam was when he was 'himself', he had blown hot and then cold so often with her. 'He's putting too many hours in,' she said, avoiding a direct answer.

'But he does that, when the mood takes him. And even so, I've never known him to be ...' Dolores paused, looking for the right word. 'Strained. He seems strained.' She was frowning again. 'Did he have some lunch?'

'I don't think he's eaten at all. I—I won't go down now, if you don't mind. Sir Charles Brouard is with him and I don't want to interrupt. In any case, I heard Adam making coffee about twenty minutes ago so they won't be ready for a drink yet.'

'Oh, dear! I do hope Adam isn't using those horrid blue mugs! He might at least have taken proper cups down if he's entertaining Sir Charles.'

Kate suppressed a smile. Adam was hardly 'entertaining'. He was working, as he had been solidly for days. Since talking to him on Monday, she had hardly seen him at all. When he'd come into the house a little earlier, she had made herself scarce. She didn't want to talk to him if she were going to have her head bitten off.

'Now what was I thinking, Kate?'

'I've no idea!'

'Oh, yes, I know.' She was patting Kate's hand, beaming now. 'I'm committed to playing bridge tonight, but tomorrow we'll all go out together. We'll go somewhere swish, mm? For your last night. I'll have words with Adam and I'll drag him out of that studio by the hair, if necessary!'

Kate thought; that's what you think. Something more drastic than that would be necessary. Adam is avoiding me, for some reason. Oh, I know he's busy, I know he's working on this commission and several other things, but he's avoiding me just the same. 'Well, if he's reluctant, you mustn't push it, Aunt Dolly. Anyway,' she smiled, 'we can have a nice dinner here, just you and me.'

'Certainly not! I'm sending you off in style, Kate. It will be a celebration of your return to health and . . .' She caught hold of her hand. 'Beauty.'

Kate smiled. No, she wasn't beautiful. But there was hope. She would have to see what the surgeon had to say. In any case, her career was not over, as she'd once thought.

Adam came into the house at nine that night. Kate didn't hear him, wasn't aware of anything until she heard his voice.

'Where's Mum?'

Kate put her book down, looking at him from some distance. He was standing in the doorway to the kitchen. 'She's out, playing bridge. It's Friday.'

'Is it?' He ran a rather dirty hand through his thick, blond hair. 'What time is it? My watch is upstairs.'

'It's almost nine. Adam——' She broke off, unsure whether or not to say what she was thinking. It was hard to judge his mood but it was obvious he was tired. Very tired. There again, why should she care?

But she did care. She couldn't stop herself. 'Can I

make you something to eat? You haven't had anything all day, have you?'

'I had breakfast.'

'Then it must have been before six this morning.'

'It was.' He came into the room and sat down. 'I hear you're leaving this weekend?'

'That's right. I got a cancellation for a flight on Sunday.'

'A cancellation? I could have flown you over myself.'

Kate smiled without humour. 'What's up? Can't you wait to get rid of me?'

'On the contrary, it seems you can't wait to go.'

'It isn't that at all. I have to go.'

'Might I ask why?'

She gaped at him. 'Why? You know very well why. I have to see the surgeon, I have to get myself together. What's the matter with you? Is your brain exhausted?'

'Something like that.' He looked directly at her for the first time since they'd been talking. 'Kate . . .'

She waited. He paused. Then he looked away, shaking his head. 'I—yes, I'd be very grateful for some food. Thanks.' He pushed himself to his feet. 'I'll have a shower first.'

'What would you like? We've got——'

'Anything.'

There it was again! He'd snapped at her. 'Adam, I don't know what I've done to upset you but——'

'You've done nothing.' He turned, his hand on the knob of the door at the far end of the room. 'You've done nothing to upset me, Kate. How could you?'

'I—don't know. But you've been avoiding me.'

'Avoiding you? What nonsense! You know damn well how much I've got on. I'm an artist, I have to work when the mood takes me, when the inspiration's there.'

'And you can't possibly be inspired just now,' she countered. 'You're absolutely whacked. You've been working throught the night and——' She broke off. As soon as the words were out, she regretted them.

'How would you know?'

She looked away. She'd invited that. 'Because—
because I've seen the lights blazing.'

'Haven't you been sleeping properly? You're not still
having that nightmare, are you?'

'No. I just—just happened to wake up in the middle
of the night, last night.'

'I see.' He gave her one last, searching look before
leaving the room.

Kate sighed with relief once he'd gone. What a fool
she was, she'd almost let herself down. No, she hadn't
been troubled with the nightmare, nor did she think she
would be again. But she hadn't been sleeping very well.
She woke up at odd times, feeling troubled and not
quite knowing why—except that Adam was constantly
on her mind. For the past few nights she had stood by
her window at various hours, looking down at the
bright lights from the roof of his studio.

'It's only sausage, egg and chips, I hope that's okay?'

'Fine. Anything's fine.' Adam sat at the table in the
breakfast nook and smiled his most charming smile.

Kate turned her attention back to the stove, her
pulses pounding. His hair was damp and apparently
darker because of it. But during the past few weeks it
had in fact grown lighter, had been bleached by the sun
until it was the colour of antique gold.

He had shed his smock and had changed into a clean
pair of denims and a white shirt which was open half
way down his chest. With his eyes closed he sat at the
table, waiting to be fed, and Kate felt a rush of
tenderness towards him. He looked so tired and yet—
and yet he looked boyish right now.

'Damn!'

'What's up?'

She turned to look at him again, grinning. 'Sorry to
wake you! I've just broken the yolk of your egg.'

Adam laughed. 'I shouldn't worry too much about

that! I'm so hungry, I won't even notice.'

She dropped another egg into the pan.

Putting his plate in front of him, she sat and sipped at a cup of coffee, amused by the way he wolfed the food down. 'More? Would you like some ice-cream or something?'

'Or something.' He smiled, caught hold of her hand and brought it to his lips. 'Thank you. That was good. And it was good of you to do it. More than I deserve.'

'How right you are.' She agreed absolutely, thinking herself crazy for pandering to him like this, trying again to harden herself against him. But the touch of his lips on her hand was doing all sorts of things to her. He was kissing her palm, inch by inch, his eyes closed in concentration. 'Adam——'

'I'm busy.'

'*Adam*. Stop that.' She pulled her hand away. 'Have you had enough to eat or not?'

'Mm. Come on, let's relax for a while. Sit yourself down in the other room and I'll make some fresh coffee. It's my turn to wait on you.'

'No. Actually, I—was just on my way to bed when you came in.'

'Rubbish! I've asked you not to tell silly lies, haven't I? Since when do you go to bed at nine forty-five?' He was glancing at his watch. 'Now who's avoiding whom?'

With a casual shrug, Kate made her way to the living-room. 'I've no reason to avoid you, Adam.'

'Haven't you?' Something in his voice made her turn to look at him. 'We're alone in the house. Can you look me in the eyes and tell me you're not worried in case I seduce you?'

Kate did precisely that. 'I'm not worried in the least.'

'You might even enjoy it.'

She walked away. 'I might at that.' Over her shoulder, she added, 'But I don't intend to find out.'

When they'd settled in the living-room, he asked, 'So

what now? You're going home to London on Sunday and—then what?'

'I'm seeing the doctor on Thursday. About the plastic surgery.'

'And when will that happen?'

'I don't know. When they can take me. Assuming that's what he advises me to do.'

'Do you feel it's worth it? The scars are so faint now——'

'Of course it's worth it!' She flared up at that. 'What an illogical question. Why should I settle for this,' she said, tapping her cheek, 'when they might be able to remove the scars completely?'

'All right, all right, keep your hair on! I'm the man who thinks you're beautiful as you are, remember?'

What could she say to that?

Adam stretched out on the settee, it was a three-seater and his legs stuck out way beyond the arm of it. God, he looked so attractive, so big and powerful and . . . Sexy. That summed it up accurately. Sexy.

'In any case,' he went on, 'there are plenty of other things you could do, besides modelling. You're an intelligent girl, Kate, I'm sure you'd be successful no matter what you turned your hand to.'

'I'm not so sure about that, but thanks for the show of faith. I might be reasonably intelligent but I'm not exactly well-educated. I left school with only three O-levels.' She shrugged. 'I wish my parents had pushed me harder, or at least encouraged me more as far as education's concerned. I was always very much the baby to them, their baby girl. They pushed my brother Thomas very hard, both of them, but never me.'

'That was a mistake.'

'I know. It's all wrong but lots of parents are like that, even today. It's a hangover from the old way of thinking—that daughters grow up and get married and are provided for.'

Adam smiled at that. 'There's nothing to stop you educating yourself, if you want to get some qualifications.'

'Agreed. But there's nothing I particularly want to do, nothing that particularly appeals. I happen to like modelling.'

'You like being in the limelight, you like that world?'

'Yes. Is that wrong?'

'No,' he said quietly. 'We're all made differently, aren't we?'

He was quiet for a while, his eyes resting on her thoughtfully.

'What are you thinking, Adam? Why are you looking at me like that?'

'I couldn't begin to tell you.' His smile was slow, audacious. 'It might make you blush. I was thinking what I'd like to do with you for the next couple of hours.'

Kate, much to her chagrin, went scarlet and looked away. She wasn't embarrassed by such remarks from the opposite sex, she was embarrassed because he'd mirrored her own thoughts. 'Aunt Dolly suggested we all go out to dinner tomorrow, for my last night. She—she wants to go somewhere swish, I quote. I don't know how you feel about it but——'

'Sounds nice. It's okay by me, if that's what she wants.'

'But is it what you want?' she challenged. 'If you'd rather work, I'll understand perfectly——'

Before she got to the end of the sentence, Adam was on his feet. 'I'll show you what I want.'

She would probably never forgive herself, but she met him more than halfway. It seemed that where he was concerned, her common sense, her will-power, simply melted away.

First they were standing, locked in each other's arms, and then they were on the settee, stretched out, hands exploring each other's bodies, their mouths hungry, meeting, separating, meeting again.

Desire swamped them both like a tidal wave; neither of them were thinking, neither of them was aware of anything but the other, the caresses, the arousal which continued to mount, to demand satisfaction. 'Kate, I want you. I can't take any more of this——'

'I want you, too,' she murmured against his mouth. 'I want you, I want you very much!' Then she was being lifted in his arms, was clinging to him, looking into brown velvet eyes which told her just how much he needed her.

It was the sound of Dolores' voice which brought the return of sanity. A harsh, shocking, cruel return. But a necessary one. One Kate was grateful for—later.

'Hello? I'm home!'

There wasn't much warning but it was enough. Dolly's voice came from the kitchen. Kate saw the look of astonishment on Adam's face just before his eyes closed briefly. Then she was back on her own two feet—but he was still holding her. 'I don't believe it,' he muttered. His lips brushed against her hair, she could feel the rapid beat of his heart as he held her close. 'Let me go, Adam, she's about to walk in!'

'So what?'

Dolly stuck her head round the door. There was the merest hint of surprise on her face when she saw them standing together in the middle of the room, Adam's arm around Kate's shoulder. 'Oh! You're both here! That's nice. Put the kettle on, would you? One of you. Must pop upstairs . . .' She vanished.

'Adam——'

'I know, I know. I'm sorry, Kate. I had no idea what time it was. Or has she come home earlier than usual?'

'No. It's getting on for midnight.' He was holding both her hands in his. She freed them, not quite knowing what to say. She regretted what had happened, she also regretted the interruption ... what the hell was the matter with her?

It was he who moved away first. He turned his back on her, one hand rubbing tiredly at the back of his neck. 'It's just as well.' He spoke in that cold voice with which she was only too familiar.

'Yes, it is.' Her tone was equally cold. 'We'd both have been riddled with regrets. There's a time and place, et cetera.'

'I didn't mean that. I'd have no regrets making love to you, here or anywhere else. I want you. But from your point of view, perhaps Dolly's homecoming was a blessing.'

'From my point of view?'

He turned to face her. 'That's what I said. Likewise, it's as well that you're leaving on Sunday.'

She wasn't following him, couldn't catch the turn of thought his mind had taken. What had she done wrong now? There was still harshness in his voice. 'I don't know what you mean, Adam.'

'I mean you're not as level-headed as I am. I mean you don't view things with the same detachment. To put it simply, I think you're in danger of falling in love with me.'

Danger. She heard the word. And oh, how very dangerous it would be, if that were the case. Fortunately, it was not. The coldness in his voice was in his eyes, too. He was looking at her now as if he were warning her off! 'My God, you certainly think a lot of yourself, don't you!' She laughed at him, an unpleasant sound. 'Falling in love? With *you*? There's not a chance of that! There never was and never could be. It's a joke!'

'Kate, Kate, listen——'

'Do me a favour!' Her voice rose. She flung herself into a chair, knowing she couldn't escape. Not now. Not tonight. Dolly would be back any second, she couldn't just take off for her room. She pushed herself out of the chair again. 'For God's sake . . . I'd better put the kettle on. As for you, you flatter yourself! What I feel for you is purely physical. Physical and meaningless. Do you know something, Mr Adam de la Mare? Your arrogance is nauseating! You're not even my type, believe it or not. There's a certain *animal* magnetism about you, granted. But it goes too far. Most of the time, I find you uncouth, not to mention unkempt!'

He took it calmly, all her quiet ranting. He seemed unmoved, neither cross nor amused. In other words, he didn't give a hoot for her opinion of him. 'I'm glad to hear it. Glad you heeded my warning.'

Kate was half way to the kitchen. She spun round. 'What warning?'

Adam merely shrugged. 'Not to let it go to your head, whatever it was you felt for me. Feel for me. I've never led you to expect anything, Kate.'

Indignation almost choked her. 'I don't believe it! You—I don't know what you're implying now, but let me assure you I have never *expected* anything of you. Or any other man, for that matter. I—oh, for heaven's sake! Don't say anything more to infuriate me, please, I can hear Dolly coming down. Act civilised, will you? Surely you can manage that until I leave? I've got one more evening to get through with you, which I will for Dolly's sake, and that's more than enough. After tomorrow, you can work yourself to a standstill. Or, preferably, you can go to hell!'

CHAPTER EIGHT

SHIVERING, Kate walked into her living-room and dumped her cases on the floor. It was warm outside but her flat felt chilly, unlived in. It looked alien to her, unwelcoming somehow.

She walked from room to room, feeling like a stranger in a strange place. Her apartment was three floors up in a smart building, and the traffic wasn't especially heavy outside but it seemed frantic today. The sounds of it roared at her through the windows, disturbing her and what should have been the silence of her home. Her home? Of course it was her home. But the place was soulless!

She felt down, depressed, as she looked around. Already she was wishing herself back on Guernsey, back in the old-fashioned but characterful, comfortable, living-room at the farmhouse.

Back where Adam was.

It seemed criminal to have to put electric fires on when it was almost June, but she had to. She was cold and she needed cheering. The central heating for the building was off, of course. Hot, cold or somewhere between, the central heating came on at the beginning of October and it went off at the end of April. And for that privilege, one paid a fortune as part of the service charge.

Maybe she would look for a new place.

A stupid thought. She'd always liked this flat before, what was she thinking about? It was modern, smart, light and airy and easy to clean.

It had no soul.

Or maybe she had no soul. She plonked herself down

heavily on a white, two-seater settee, stuck her feet on a tubular steel coffee table topped with glass, and took a good look around.

It was she who had decorated the place, she who had furnished it, she alone who was responsible for the way it looked. Lord, was she really so unimaginative?

It was a long time before she could find enough enthusiasm to get up and make a hot drink. She stood by the window with a cup of coffee, looking down. What a contrast! How noisy, dirty, grimy everything seemed. After the lovely view from her aunt's house, the sea, the open fields, the fresh air she had spent so much time in, she wondered whether she'd ever adjust to London again. Everything seemed so—so colourless.

She sat, thinking, brooding, getting cross and then calming down again. Plotting and planning and then changing her mind, telling herself that her future was in the lap of the gods. And the hands of the doctor.

Her future and her looks occupied only a tiny proportion of her thinking. It was Adam who dominated her thoughts.

So what else was new?

Her last, *final*, evening with him had been a shambles. Aunt Dolly, loving and lovable Aunt Dolly, had kept the small party going in her usual fashion. If she had sensed the atmosphere between her niece and her stepson, she had given no sign of it. But then she wouldn't, would she? It wasn't her style. Bless her.

They had gone to dinner at the Victor Hugo restaurant in the St Pierre Park, Guernsey's newest hotel, and its swishest. Adam and she had sat facing one another, being polite, being ever so civilised, saying nothing. Afterwards, he had changed into his working clothes and had vanished.

He hadn't seen her off at the airport; he'd left Dolores to do that, alone. Rather, he'd slept late. He'd still been in bed when Kate left.

So much for him.

But why, why did it hurt so much? After all, she had told the truth when she'd said he wasn't even her type. Basically, he wasn't. She had always been attracted to the executive type, the snappy dresser, the sophisticated type of man who took her to sophisticated places. It was only fitting; she was a sophisticated girl, wasn't she?

Wasn't she?

Perhaps. Once. She was no longer sure. It seemed she was no longer sure of anything, of her own image, her own needs, no longer sure what she wanted from life. The forthcoming operation seemed unimportant. Maybe Adam had been right in asking her whether it was worth having. Was it? For the sake of her photographic modelling career? Or for her self-esteem. Yes, it was worth it for her self-esteem. She needed to get that back in full measure.

Adam de la Mare had managed somehow, finally, to rob her of some of that. How dared he imply she would be a clinging vine—or something? How dared he say she was in danger of falling in love with him, as if she were a starry-eyed schoolgirl who was unsure of her own mind? And to think of his arrogance! Warning her off like that! Who the hell did he think he was? And another thing . . . how dared he—he . . .

She was crying again.

She was sobbing this time, great, racking sobs which tore through her until she was hiccupping and blowing her nose and crying all at the same time.

It was only then that she realised how accurate Adam had been.

She had fallen in love with him long since.

Harley Street was as busy as usual, private cars and taxis were coming and going, unloading passengers who went privately to doctors in the old and well cared for buildings. Fine buildings with polite, discreet, ultra-smart receptionists. Brass name plates. No mention of money. The bill would be sent at the end of the month. Harley Street the famous.

Kate wouldn't have gone anywhere else.

She looked at the highly-polished name plate and rang the appropriate bell. Four minutes later she was ushered from the hushed, luxurious atmosphere of the waiting room and was face to face with the man who might or might not recommend surgery. She hadn't met him before; she had been referred to him by the doctor in Bristol. This man was a specialist, a Mr Frederick Kempton-Jones, FRCS.

On his desk was her letter of referral, and Kate waited, weighing him up. He looked kindly, he was fifty-ish and slim for his age, immaculate, grey haired, blue-eyed. Kate's eyes shifted to his hands, wondering quite how capable and skilled they were.

'Well, Miss Sumner,' he said at length. 'Let's take a look at you, shall we?'

She was out on the street again half an hour later. It was all arranged. She would be admitted to a private nursing home, a different one from last time, on Tuesday of next week. The operation would take place on Wednesday. It was as fast and as easy as that. Moreover Mr Frederick Kempton-Jones, one of the best surgeons in his field, had promised that her face would look precisely, exactly, as it used to look, that when the bandages were removed after so many days, she would be her old self. One hundred per cent. It was, he had said, a simple procedure.

She ought to have been thrilled.

'*Kate!* Hey, Kate!'

She spun round, trying to decide which direction the voice had come from. She knew the voice, it was that of Marliyn Cross, no doubt about that. It was the one thing that spoiled Marilyn, that rather shrill, often giggly voice. Marilyn: co-model, colleague, friend. Well, colleague at any rate.

'Kate, Kate, you're back! Where've you been, for heaven's sake? And why didn't you let us know where you were? I spoke to your Mum on the phone and——' As the other girl came to a halt at Kate's side, she gaped. 'Kate! Why, you look fine!'

'Marilyn——'

'No, I'm not just being kind. Honestly, I'd been led to believe your face was wrecked.'

'It was.' Kate couldn't help smiling. 'My cheekbone was shattered but they glued it together again. Or something. Nature did the rest. It's not too bad, is it?'

'It's a bloody relief to me, I'll tell you that much!' She linked her arm through Kate's. 'Come on, let's get a cup of coffee somewhere. Have you called in at the agency yet?'

Kate hadn't been out, she had stayed at home, pining. 'No, I haven't been out till today, except for some groceries.'

'Wait till Marcia sees you! There's loads of work around just now.'

'Hang on. Weren't you on your way somewhere?'

'I've just been.' Marilyn wrinkled her nose, her blonde hair cascading around her shoulders as she shook her head in distaste. 'To the dentist's. Just for a clean, thank goodness. Still, I hate it!'

Kate was virtually being frog-marched down the street. 'Oh, Kate, we've all been so worried about you, honestly. It was mean of you not to let anyone know where you were. Getting your parents to put the block on! Why did you do that?'

When they'd settled themselves in a café, Kate apologised. Marilyn's greeting had been so warm and friendly, her concern seemed genuine enough. Perhaps Adam was right, perhaps she'd been callous in her thinking, not giving people a chance to show their friendship. 'I—first, let me apologise. And I want to thank you for the flowers you sent, and your letter. It's just that—well, I suppose I was in shock, not thinking straight. I imagined everyone would either weep and wail as my mother did, or that people wouldn't know what to say to me. I thought my life was over, Marilyn, I know it seems dramatic now but——'

'It's all right.' Her hand was covered, squeezed. 'I don't know what I'd have done in the circumstances. But what about Roger?' Marilyn's tone changed. 'It was wrong of you not to let him see you. Granted, I didn't come to the nursing home myself because—well, in a way you're right, I wouldn't have known what the hell to say to you. I wouldn't have known how to comfort you. But it's different with Roger. I've seen him around and he's as miserable as sin. Don't you realise he feels responsible?'

'Responsible?'

'For the accident, for course. After all, he was driving.'

'But it wasn't his fault!' Kate felt awful. It hadn't been Roger's fault, not at all. 'A motorcycle crashed into us, it shot over the junction without stopping——'

'I know all that. For pity's sake, ring him, Kate. Will you?'

'Yes, of course.'

'Promise?'

'Marilyn, I've just said——' Kate shut up abruptly. She couldn't blame her friend for doubting her. She had behaved oddly, perhaps selfishly. 'Have you got time for lunch?'

'You bet. But let's go somewhere nicer than this?'

'You are eating today then?' Kate was laughing. Marilyn was on a permanent diet. Come to think of it, she'd always been on a diet herself. Not a drastic one, she didn't need to do that, but she had always watched her figure carefully. She was eight pounds heavier now than she'd been when she got to Guernsey—but so what?

'What's the matter?' Marilyn saw the change in Kate's eyes. Those fabulous eyes of hers could tell their own story.

'Nothing.'

'You're talking to me, remember? Your big blue eyes have gone dark, darling. What's up? Is it a man?'

'A man?' Kate had to deny it, she didn't want to think about Adam, let alone talk of him. 'No. I've lived . . . very much like a hermit for weeks. With my aunt.'

'Whatever for?'

'Because—because it was a long time before I realised my face wasn't as hideous as I thought it was.'

'Oh, Kate! You idiot. It looks——' She leaned closer, screwed up her eyes a little. 'Well, it isn't what it was, I have to be honest. Unless they can do something for you, your photographic days are over. But you can always model clothes. *Can't* they do something? I'd have thought that these days——'

'Oh, yes.' Kate almost waved the subject away. 'I'm having plastic surgery next week. I've been promised a miracle, complete success. The surgeon seems to think it'll be a doddle.'

'*Kate!*' Marilyn was squeaking again. 'That's marvellous. Oh, I can't tell you how glad that makes me!'

And she really meant it. Ashamed of herself, Kate insisted on paying for lunch. It was the least she could do.

She let herself into her flat during the early evening, around five. Having spent a couple of hours with Marilyn, she'd gone to see Marcia Holman, who owned and managed the modelling agency she worked for. Marcia's reaction had been similar to Marilyn's. 'So you'll soon be back in the swing of things? Super! How super!'

Was it? Then why did she feel so empty?

At six on the dot, as if by prior arrangement, Roger presented himself on Kate's doorstep. Tall, dark and handsome, immaculate as ever. He didn't look pleased, he looked angry. 'So you're back? You might have let me know. I had to hear it from Marilyn. She had the goodness to phone me this afternoon, why didn't you?'

'Roger, I—come in.' Rather than lie, she said nothing. The truth was, she'd forgotten all about him.

He followed her into the living-room, going on. And on. 'Have you any idea how I've been feeling? I mean, can you imagine what I've been through? When your mother refused point blank to tell me where you were, I couldn't believe it! I didn't think you had it in you, Kate.'

'I'm sorry, honestly I am. Let me get you a drink. What will you have?'

'You know I don't drink!' He looked at her as though she'd gone mad. Why should she have remembered? It was hardly paramount in her thoughts. She'd known the man for some time, by sight to begin with, but she'd only dated him for three months.

Three months. It was enough time in which to learn a person's preferences and habits. It was time enough in which to fall in love.

More than enough.

'Shall I make you a coffee then?'

'No, don't bother.' Roger sat down, seemingly pacified. But he wasn't. A moment later he started again. 'I've been thinking all sorts of things. I thought you'd emigrated or something! Not a phone call, not a word—nothing. How bloody thoughtless can you get?'

Kate poured herself a drink. He was beginning to get on her nerves. 'Look, let me make myself absolutely clear on at least one thing, Roger; in no way do I hold you responsible for the accident. You were in no way to blame.'

'I know that.'

'Then what's all the fuss about?'

He was looking at her as if he didn't know her at all. Perhaps he didn't. 'What's happened to you? You're— different. And I'm not talking about your face, which, by the way, isn't half as bad as I'd expected.'

'Thank you.' He missed the irony in her voice. She wanted to change the subject. Either that, or he would have to go. Forcing a smile, she gave him the once-over. He was as smart, as spotless as ever in his pin-stripe suit and immaculate shirt. 'You're looking well, Roger. How's the stock market?'

He was staring at her now. 'The stock market? Never mind the stock market! Where have you been all these months?'

'On Guernsey.'

'Guernsey?'

'One of the Channel Islands.'

Roger's face went pink. 'I'm well aware of its geography! But why? Why did you take off? And what's the attraction on Guernsey, it's just a dot of a place, isn't it?'

Very calmly she told him the island had many attractions. Naturally she made no mention of Adam. 'I wanted to hide . . .' She went through it all again, that which she'd said to Marilyn earlier in the day.

'All right,' he said at length, 'I see your point. So how are you feeling now?'

'Why Roger, I thought you'd never ask!'

'Are you being sarcastic, Kate?'

'Yes.' She got up, helped herself to another drink from the stainless steel and glass bar in the corner. 'I've finished explaining myself. I didn't really owe you an explanation to begin with. Just in case you've forgotten, it was you who suggested we didn't see each other for a while.'

'I meant—for heaven's sake, you make me feel ashamed. I only meant a couple of weeks. You were in such a state, I thought you'd be better on your own, I thought you needed time to adjust.'

'I see.'

'I don't think you do. I'm in love with you.'

She was smiling, a beautiful, sad sort of smile. 'All I can say to that is, you have a funny way of showing it.'

'I wasn't given the chance.'

'You're contradicting yourself.'

'I meant at the nursing home. You wouldn't let me see you.'

'You didn't try very hard. And I was very much in need of reassurance, support.'

Roger looked heavenward. 'Women! I haven't met one yet who was easy to please. You complain because I didn't insist on seeing you at the nursing home, you complain because I kept away, and now you're complaining because I suggested we didn't see each other for a while! What's it all about, Kate?'

It had to stop. This was pointless. 'That's easy enough to work out, isn't it? You don't really love me, Roger. And I'm glad of that, because I'm not in love with you, I never came even close to it.'

His face was red now. He got up, his voice very quiet as he told her he was aware of that. 'But I do love you. I might not understand all your emotional needs, but I am in love with you. And one can hope. I know you were seeing other men while you were dating me but— what is it with you now? You are different, and I can't work out what it is. Have you—did you meet someone while you were away?'

'I met lots of people.'

'Kate——'

'I'm sorry.' She sighed. She really was sorry. 'You'd better go, Roger. If you stay, I'll end up hurting you more. I don't mean to, but I know I will, somehow.'

'But—I thought we might go out to dinner?'

'No. I'm tired. I'm really very tired. I'm not going out at all till I'm over this operation.'

He saw that she meant it. 'May I ring you?'

'If you want to.'

'Marilyn says you're going into hospital next week, is that right?'

Kate nodded. 'On Tuesday.' She held out her hand to him. He put it to his lips. She made no effort to stop him. 'Yes, I'll be in for about ten days. Ring me when I come home, if you want to know how I am.'

'I want more than that, Kate. I—all right.' Wisely, he left it at that for the moment.

Kate tried to relax when he'd gone. She couldn't. She moved around restlessly. She had to ring her parents and tell them of the arrangements she'd made, tell them what the surgeon had said. That was fine, but—but she had to ring Aunt Dolly, too. She must. It was only right and proper.

She phoned her parents first. She also phoned her brother, who lived in Southampton. Then she could put it off no longer. She drained her glass, picked up the receiver and dialled Guernsey.

Please God, don't let Adam answer the phone, I couldn't handle it.

He didn't.

CHAPTER NINE

'THERE'S a visitor for you, Kate. A man.'

Kate's heart leapt into her throat. A visitor? Male? She wasn't expecting anyone today. Her mother had come to see her yesterday, her father was coming tomorrow because he was going to be in London in any case. So who was here now? 'What—who is it?' Hardly able to get the question out, her hand moved to touch the bandages on her face. It wouldn't be, couldn't be ... Adam. Could it? Was it possible?

The day nurse, with whom Kate had become quite friendly, was smiling. 'I've told you, a man. A handsome one at that. I didn't ask his name. He's outside, shall I send him in?'

'No!' At the look on the nurse's face, she added, 'I mean, I mean—not until I know who it is. I——' If some sort of miracle had happened, if it were Adam, she would have to compose herself before she faced him. 'What does he look like?'

'Worried.' Cathy Mansfield giggled. She was around Kate's age and she was as cheerful as she was efficient. 'Tall and dark, beautifully dressed. He looks like a stockbroker.'

Kate's heart dropped like a stone. What a fool she had been to hope ... She should have known straight away that it was Roger. Adam could not be described as handsome. His face was too—too craggy, too interesting to be merely handsome. Good-looking, certainly, but she wouldn't describe him as handsome. 'That's precisely what he is,' she said dully, fighting against the threat of tears. 'Tell him to go away, Cathy.'

134

The nurse frowned. 'Are you sure?'

'Absolutely.'

Cathy was back in less than a minute. 'He says he isn't going to take no for an answer.' There was a big grin. 'That's what I like, the assertive type. If I were you——'

'Assertive?' Kate almost laughed at that. 'If you think Roger's assertive, you should meet——' She broke off, wanting to bite out her tongue. 'Never mind. Please tell him he arranged to phone me, not to visit me here. I will not see him, and that's that. Don't look so concerned, he'll go away without any further fuss.'

Roger left without further fuss. Ten minutes later Cathy was back. 'There's someone else to see you now. Popular today, aren't we?'

'A man?' Fool, fool! She was doing it again!

'A little old lady. Well, elderly, I should say. Mrs de la Mare. She says she's your aunt.'

Kate's hand flew to her mouth.

'What's the matter now? Don't you want to see your aunt, either?'

'*Yes!* Send her in!' If Dolores were here, surely, surely, Adam was here, too? At least, if not here at the nursing home, he must be in London. He must have brought Dolores in his plane.

'Aunt Dolly! Oh, how lovely to see you! How kind of you to come. All this way . . .'

'Carnations from Guernsey!' Aunt Dolly waved a big bunch of gaily coloured carnations under Kate's nose, provoking all sorts of memories for her. In those few seconds she was strolling along the lanes in St Pierre du Bois once more in the early hours, listening to the gulls, the occasional bleat of a sheep, enjoying the solitude, the very air she was breathing. So much, so very much had happened to her in the space of three months . . .

She couldn't speak.

'Would you take these, please, dear?' Dolores handed

the flowers to Cathy, who was hovering, looking at her patient with a hint of concern.

'Thanks, Cathy.' Kate forced herself to speak, to show she was all right.

'Kate. How are you, dear?' Aunt Dolly held out her arms and Kate moved into them. She was hugged gently, carefully. 'When are those bandages coming off?'

'They're not taking them off until Friday, so I have to be patient for five more days.' It was Monday today. 'Oh, Aunt Dolly, I'm so pleased to see you! I've missed you. How sweet of you to come all this way, again! Did—did Adam bring you?'

'No. I travelled with him, but on a commercial flight. We flew to Heathrow.'

So he was in London! There was hope! Surely he'd call in? He couldn't be in London and not pop in to say hello? Could he? He'd be calling to collect Dolores after her visit. She would see him then. Oh, God, it had been less than three weeks since she'd seen him but they had been the longest days of her life. Here, lying day after day in the hospital, she had nothing to distract her mind from the pain of missing him. Not for one minute had he been out of her thoughts.

'May I sit on the bed?' Aunt Dolly was asking. 'I thought I'd kill two birds, so to speak. I thought I'd visit you and then spend a couple of days with Anne and George. I'll take the train up to Bristol after I leave here. They're expecting me.'

'Mum didn't say anything about this yesterday.'

'It was only arranged last night. I decided on impulse to travel to London with Adam. I have to confess,' she added, with a somewhat guilty look on her face, 'I wouldn't go on to Bristol if Adam were still at home. Someone has to make sure he eats, sometime! But there's nothing I can do about that while he's in New York, is there?'

'New—New York?'

'Mm. I've just left him at Heathrow. He'll be on his way now.'

'I . . . see.'

'He's going on Concorde, isn't that exciting?'

'I wouldn't know, I've never flown on Concorde. What's he—how long will he be there?'

'About three weeks. A very important gallery,' she added, very importantly, 'is doing a major show of his work. Adam will be there for the preview and he's also doing some teaching sessions with a few sculptors who are already making names for themselves. A sort of master-class,' she added proudly.

The only response Kate could manage was a nod. Dolores had every right to be proud of Adam; he was a very gifted man and his fame and fortune had not yet reached its peak. But she couldn't enthuse. She loved Adam de la Mare the man, not the sculptor. Much as she admired his work, much as she was interested in it, his being a famous sculptor had never gone to her head, never overly impressed her; she knew quite a few famous people. Still, his art did fascinate her, she and Adam had spent time together in his studio, Kate asking questions about technicalities, Adam patiently answering them. In fact, there wasn't much she didn't know about, for instance, plaster casting!

Heaven help me, she thought, wanting to cry.

Why she loved him, how it had happened, she had no idea. They could hardly have got off to a worse start; she had hated him to begin with but—but there it was. 'Did he finish that bust of Sir Charles?'

'Yes, but it hasn't been cast. Adam said he's not satisfied with it, though Sir Charles thinks it's marvellous as it is.' Dolores shrugged. 'I'm a bit worried about him, to tell you the truth.'

'Sir Charles? Do you know him that well?'

'Yes, actually. But I didn't mean him, you silly girl! I

was talking about Adam. He's been like a bear with a
sore head since you left.' She looked very pointedly at
her niece. 'What does it mean, Kate? Is there something
I ought to know?'

'Nothing at all. He was like a bear with a sore head
when I was there. Or have you forgotten?'

Dolly's next words left Kate open-mouthed. 'Well, I
don't know, I'm sure. But I'll tell you this, if he comes
back from New York in the same peculiar mood, an
aggressive sort of mood, I'm going to give him a piece
of my mind!'

Kate bit into her cheeks. It was the first time she had
ever heard her aunt speak harshly about her stepson.
Normally she defended him to a ridiculous extent.
What a turn up! 'He's going back to Guernsey then,
after New York?'

'For a while. He has to organise the shipment of
some of his work. I'm not sure where to. It's a tricky
business, you can imagine, and he wouldn't trust
anyone else to handle it in his absence.'

Kate felt more miserable than ever when her aunt
left. Knowing that Adam was on the other side of the
world made things seem even more hopeless.

Even more hopeless? What *was* she hoping for? How
pathetic could she get? There had never been any hope
for anything in the first place. Adam had made that
excruciatingly clear. More than once. Was this what she
was reduced to now? To being a day-dreamer? Was this
what being in love did to you?

No! Not to her. She wasn't going to fall to pieces.
Not any more than she already had. Not any *longer*!
Once she was out of this nursing home, she would be,
to use Marcia's words, back in the swing of things. As
quickly as possible. There were many, many men out
there, and she was going to be beautiful again. There
were shows to see, parties to go to, restaurants to eat in,
discos to dance in. It was her world. She was going

back to the days of wine and roses. No, it would be even better than that! She would make sure of it. She was going to paint the town red, she was going to have Champagne days!

Marilyn Cross came to visit that evening. On Tuesday evening some of the other girls from the agency turned up. On Wednesday Marilyn turned up again, with the owner of the agency, Marcia Holman. They were both armed with books and flowers and fruit.

It was someone to talk to, at least, better than lying there alone in the room, pretending to read while she was really thinking about Adam.

She talked too much that evening. Over the past few days, her resolve to get out and about had hardened. So determined was she to be her old self, her old fun-loving self, she got over-enthusiastic. 'I can't *wait* to get out of here! I miss the parties, have done for ages. Not to mention the fellers!'

'Speaking of which,' Marilyn's smile faded somewhat, 'why didn't you see Roger today? That's twice he's tried to see you, he came here on Monday and then again today. Why did you send him away—again?'

'Hey, what's going on? What's the matter with you? It's over between me and Roger. It never really got started.' As realisation dawned, Kate smiled. 'You fancy him yourself, is that it? Well, Marilyn darling, help yourself!'

'He's in love with you, you idiot.'

'No, he isn't. He doesn't know the meaning of the word. Perhaps you can teach him, Marilyn? You're obviously keen, you've been ringing him. You must have, if you know he's been here twice.'

'I asked him out,' Marilyn admitted, shrugging. 'Which is hardly the way I usually go about things. He had the gall to refuse!' She tried to laugh it off.

'*You* asked *him* out?' Marcia couldn't believe it. 'You? And he said no?'

'You can't win 'em all, Marcia.'

Kate might have said that herself. No, one couldn't. The irony was that the one man she wanted to win, had ever wanted to win, was uninterested to the point of warning her off, to the point of sending her not so much as a single flower or a get-well card. He hadn't even sent his regards; Aunt Dolly had conveyed no message at all from him. Well, let him go to hell!

Which was all very well, thinking like that, but the feeling always passed. She did have moments when she resented Adam so much she felt she hated him. It passed. Love and hate, as they say, are often very closely intertwined. She knew what people meant by that now.

'I have a girl with a battered ego on my hands,' Marcia was saying to Kate, referring, of course, to Marilyn. 'What can we do about it?'

'Have fun! Get out and meet new people. That's what I'm going to do, soon as I've got rid of this bed. I'm bored to death in here. In fact I don't know why they've kept me in, I'm perfectly well in myself, I'm just waiting for the day of the bandages.'

'When is it?'

'The day after tomorrow. Keep fingers crossed.'

'It'll be all right.' Marcia crossed her fingers nevertheless. 'It had better be. There's a lot of work coming in your direction, as soon as you're circulating again.'

'I'm glad to hear it.' Kate was lying. She couldn't care less. Still, she had to earn a living. Didn't she have a smart and desirable apartment to keep up? The very thought of going back to that place was depressing. She shook herself, remembering her resolve. 'Marilyn, stop looking so serious. If at first you don't succeed, and all that. Leave it a couple of days and ring Roger again, if you're really that keen. Ask him round for a meal, home-cooked, mind you, and offer him a shoulder to

cry on. He'll come round—in every sense. And good
luck to you when he does. I'll give you about three
months together.'

'What do you mean? And then what?'

'And then you'll discover that basically he's selfish.
Wholly concerned with self, egotistical. Not only that,
he's boring. You'll see.'

'Maybe, maybe not. One man's meat . . . Mind you, I
must say his car's part of his attraction! Have you seen
it, his new Ferrari?'

'I'm not interested.' Kate had a sudden mental
picture of a battered pick-up truck, could hear Adam
saying, 'Get behind the wheel, Kate. I said *get behind
the wheel*, you're driving.'

'Kate?' It was a chorus.

She blinked, she'd almost forgotten the girls were
there. 'Sorry, I was just thinking about—about my aunt
in Guernsey. She was so good to me . . .'

Marilyn rolled her eyes. 'You must have been bored
stiff, staying there. I don't know how you stuck it so
long.'

'You're right. I was bored stiff.' She bit hard into her
tongue, wishing they would go now. Where would it
end? She'd started telling bare-faced lies now . . .

'Good morning, Miss Sumner, and how are we today?'

Mr Frederick Kempton-Jones sat himself elegantly
on the side of her bed. Over his shoulder, Kate caught
the wink Cathy Mansfield gave her. Cathy was standing
to attention; it was Friday morning and the big boss
had come to do the unveiling.

'Scared.'

'Oh, ye of little faith! Come on now, sit up and we'll
see what we shall see.'

Kate braced herself, thinking: it's a wonder he didn't
add 'shall we?' But he was a sweet man with a
reassuring bedside manner. She sat perfectly still, her

heart tripping in her breast, as he slowly unwound the bandages.

Kate kept her eyes fixed firmly on his. They told her nothing. He was looking at her face with total impartiality, grunting now and then, a very refined sort of grunt, his fingers on her chin, turning her head this way and that.

At length, when she thought she could stand it no longer, he said, 'And there we have it! See what you think. Nurse . . .'

Cathy was grinning like a Cheshire cat. She stepped forward, a mirror in her hand. Kate took it from her, took a deep breath, and finally looked at herself. She hadn't seen the whole of her face since the day of her admission.

She was restored. There she was, in the mirror. Apart from two pinkish, extremely fine hairline scars, she looked exactly as she used to look.

'Don't worry about those.' The surgeon ran a finger delicately over the two tiny lines. 'They'll be invisible within a few days.'

Kate nodded, she knew without doubt the two scars would be invisible. She had remarkable healing skin; after the way she'd healed before, these would be no problem at all. She was still looking at herself, not knowing what to say. Naturally she was pleased by what she saw. But in honesty she couldn't pretend to be overjoyed. At least, she couldn't pretend to herself. It just—just didn't seem all that important any more.

Of course she couldn't tell the surgeon that. He and Cathy were waiting, watching her expectantly. 'I'm—I can't believe it. It is a miracle!' She fired her voice with enthusiasm and was rewarded with big smiles. 'Thank you, thank you—more than I can say!'

Mr Kempton-Jones nodded, still smiling as he got to his feet. Cathy wasn't so restrained. 'You're beautiful!'

she said. 'Really beautiful.'

The doctor grunted at that. 'An accurate observation, Nurse. But for the record, I thought Miss Sumner rather beautiful in the first place.'

Fortunately, the tears which sprang to Kate's eyes were misunderstood. There was nothing she could do to stop them, they just rolled down her cheeks of their own accord, a steady stream of them.

Mr Kempton-Jones was moved to the extent that he patted her hand. 'It's a normal reaction. Well, my dear, you are discharged forthwith. Good luck to you in everything you do.'

'Th-thank you.'

'Nurse . . .' Exit doctor, exit nurse, on his heels.

Kate got very maudlin very quickly. Adam. Adam! You thought I was beautiful, too. As I was. If only you'd liked what was *inside*, if only you felt the same way about me, the person.

They had left the mirror on the bedside cabinet. She picked it up and stared at her face, whispering, 'All the King's horses and all the King's men . . .'

She was sobbing when Cathy came back.

'Kate!'

'I'm all right. Honestly, Cathy, I'm all right.' Her face was buried in the pillows. She felt the other girl's arm around her shoulder.

'No, you're not. Let me see you. Come on, look at me, you shouldn't be crying this hard.'

Kate did as she was asked, making an enormous effort to control herself. 'Just tears of happiness, Cathy, they're just tears of relief and joy.'

'No.' Nurse Mansfield was not only professional, she was also a friend in that moment, a contemporary. A woman. She was shaking her head. 'No, Kate, there's more to it than that. Why don't you tell me what's on your mind?'

'I—can't. Forgive me. I appreciate what you're doing

and you've been more than kind, but—I don't want to talk about it.'

There was a swift hug, an understanding nod. 'That's okay. Just tell me it's not disappointment. You're not worrying about those little scars, are you? I promise you, I swear, you won't be able to see them in a few days. They'll have faded and——'

'I know, I know. No, it isn't that.'

Kate spoke with a finality which was the nurse's cue to leave. 'All right. Just rest for a bit and I'll come and help you get your things together. Is anyone coming for you?'

'No. Which is how I want it. I'm taking a taxi home.'

She left the hospital an hour later.

A new woman.

She was nothing like the person she used to be.

Staring out of the taxi's windows, she wondered whether she would ever feel happy again. Would she ever get used to London again? It seemed like a madhouse. The hustle and bustle was almost frightening. The taxi drove at a rate of knots. Drivers didn't wave politely to one another here, didn't stop to give way, they made rude signs and swore under their breath.

Walking into her cold-looking, empty apartment was awful. She wished she had asked someone to come for her at the nursing home; she needed company now, someone, anyone . . . 'Right! That's *it*!' In her bedroom Kate looked at her watch. It was two thirty-five. She was going to make two phone calls. The first would be to her mother, to reassure her—which would also reassure Aunty Dolly, who was still in Bristol. The second call would be to Kevin Dean. Or maybe to Giles Sommerville. Possibly Alan Milner. Maybe she would have to ring all three before she got herself invited out to dinner. After all, it was short notice and all three of them were highly eligible.

She was asked out instantly by the first one she got

through to. Kevin was not in his office; Giles Sommerville was—in his studios.

Lucky Giles!

'Hi! Guess who?'

'*Kate!* Darling! Long time, no see. I've heard the news on the grapevine. You're out of hospital, I take it? How did it go?'

'How would you like to see for yourself?' she asked, putting a smile into her voice. Giles was a photographer, a friend, one of the crowd.

'We-ell! At last! And how many times have you given me the cold-shoulder in the past? My cameras have had love-affairs with you—I just wish I could say the same! You don't need to give me more than one green light, Baby Doll, what time shall I pick you up?'

'Eight.'

'Make it seven. And dress *up*, darling.' There was a sudden laugh, an odd remark before he hung up. 'Because you don't know what you're in for tonight!'

Nor did she. She ended up wishing she'd never phoned Giles. Still, if it hadn't been him, it would have been someone else ... there was a conspiracy afoot, though she didn't know it then.

Giles arrived two minutes early. On seeing him, she wondered why she'd bothered, really. His appearance was too way out for her liking. Modern though she was, she didn't care for men who wore earrings, even if it were just the one. Nor did she think a purple shirt went with pink trousers. Not these shades, anyway. Slung over his shoulder was a camera, not that that was unusual. Giles never went anywhere without a camera.

'Giles! You look—different.'

'And you look *fabulous*!' He was staring at her face. 'Amazing! Amazing! Amazing! Marilyn told me the whole thing had been exaggerated but—it's *you*! Wow! What else can I say?'

Kate was swept into his arms and whirled round. One

of the nice things about Giles was his height. He was very tall and broad and ... and she must concentrate on him. He was going to take her out of herself tonight. He was going to make her forget. And yet she resented having his hands on her even for this friendliest of gestures. 'Hey! Put me down, will you?' She kept her voice light, laughing. 'Would you have a little consideration for the dress, please?'

The dress. Kate had spent a fortune on it. She had bought it a week before the accident and had worn it only once. It was white silk, sleeveless, low-necked and ultra-sophisticated because of its very simplicity. She had piled her hair carefully on top of her head—wearing it up for the first time since the car crash. She was showing off her face, the face which had appeared on dozens of magazine covers. And she had dressed *up* as instructed. Tonight she was the Kate Sumner everyone knew. Her make-up was immaculate, just a bit dramatic in keeping with the rest of her appearance tonight, and she had gone to town with her accessories. She was wearing the gold earrings her parents had given to her for her twenty-first, on her wrist was the dress-watch Roger had given to her that night, at her throat was a gold necklace. Her high-heeled sandals were gold, too. Tonight she was a lady in gold and white, tonight she was glamorous. Tonight she was the Kate Sumner everyone knew.

'Where are we going, Giles?'

'Wait and see!' He was grinning from ear to ear. 'You're in for a surprise, Baby Doll!'

That wasn't the impression she got when, an hour later she found herself sitting in a quiet, Italian restaurant, feeling deflated and over-dressed. 'Giles dear, would you mind telling me why you've brought me here? I don't want to sound ungrateful, and the food's marvellous but—I feel like a Christmas tree.'

'We're going on to a party.'

'Ahh!'

They were back at her flat at nine-thirty. Giles
brought his car to a halt in the residents' car park, and
only then did Kate feel a flash of alarm. What had she
done? What had she led him to *expect*? A private little
party for two, was that what he had in mind? 'Giles, I
don't understand——'

'Relax. I put my camera on your hall table and I
forgot to pick it up again. Come on, it'll only take a
minute.'

She got out of the car. It was a beautiful June
evening, warm and velvety. 'Good evening, John.' She
flashed a smile at the hall porter, who touched his cap,
beaming at her.

''Evening Miss Sumner. It's nice to see you looking
so well. 'Evening to you too, sir.'

Kate frowned. Now why should the hall porter be
winking at Giles like that? Very odd! She shrugged,
pushed the button for the lift. It was already on the
ground floor and the doors opened immediately.

They got to the third floor and turned left along the
carpeted corridor. Apart from the traffic which could
be heard even in the building's interior, all was quiet.

Kate fished for her key in the small gold evening bag
she'd taken with her and opened her door—to be met
by a sudden blaze of lights, the flashing of cameras, a
sea of faces, the joined voices of what sounded like
hundreds.

'Surprise!'

It seemed as if everyone were there, neighbours she
didn't really know very well, friends in the form of
photographers and other models, a few more friends,
the staff of the agency and, of course, Marcia and her
husband. And Marilyn. And Roger. And a couple of
reporters she knew, one of whom she'd been out with
several times. And Cathy was there, standing nearest to
her, looking very pretty with her dark hair down, more

slender, almost unrecognisable out of her nurse's uniform.

In reality there were around four dozen people. It just seemed as if the whole of London were crammed into the flat. Kate couldn't believe it. Nor did she want this. But she played the part, she had no choice. She smiled, she enthused, she thanked them all as they crowded around her, wishing her well, saying nice things about her face, welcoming her back to the fold . . .

Here she was.

Back in her world.

'To Kate!' Champagne corks were popping, music started up, live music from a few musician friends who had brought their instruments. The air was already thick with smoke, her furniture had been re-arranged, dozens of bottles were stacked on top of the bar, her glass dining table was covered with food, all her crockery and her best glasses were out, the half-dozen fancy candles she'd bought with the intention of keeping were lit. She wanted to scream. She wanted to throw all of them out.

'Thank you!' she shouted instead, laughing gaily. 'Thank you all! How marvellous! What a lovely surprise!'

She accepted the glass of champagne being thrust at her, and another, and another. She answered the bombardment of questions, similiar questions from everyone. When she had a moment in which to breathe, she went in search of Giles.

He was in the kitchen, talking to two girls. They were twins, also models. 'Giles, there you are! How did you *do* this? How—when was it organised?'

'I can't take the credit, I'm afraid. I was just the red herring, the one who got you off the premises.'

'But—but what if I hadn't phoned you?'

'Then I'd have phoned you. Or someone would. We're all in it, Kate. It's Marilyn's doing, she's the brains behind the scheme!'

Marilyn. Who else? 'But—I mean, I only got out of the nursing home today. What if I'd felt tired, what if I'd insisted I was staying in tonight?'

'But you didn't, did you?' Giles laughed his head off at the idea. 'You've got to be kidding! On the day you got your gorgeous face back? Do you think we didn't realise a celebration was called for? That you'd have wanted to stay in? What?' His laughter increased. 'With a good book for company?'

Oh, if only she had!

'You're right!' She was on her fourth glass of champagne and she giggled. It wasn't real. She was in fact stone cold sober. 'Excuse me, I must circulate.'

She turned to see Cathy Mansfield watching her from the doorway. She was looking concerned. 'I hope this wasn't a mistake, Kate? How are you feeling?'

'Great!'

Cathy looked dubious, more concerned. 'I don't know that I believe you. I've known about this for the past few days. Your friend Marilyn told me what she'd been up to and she invited me to come——'

'And you're more than welcome, Cathy. It's nice to have you here.' She glanced over her shoulder at Giles. 'Hey, you! How did everyone get in here? You must have bribed the hall porter! No wonder he was winking at you! Thank God that's all it was!'

'They didn't, actually.' Cathy was biting her lip now. 'Nobody bribed the porter.' She fished in the small leather bag she wore over her shoulder. 'Your father gave me your spare key when he came to see you the other day. He—I told him what was going on because I wanted to see what he thought of the idea. I mean, not knowing you, I didn't know how you'd react. He thought it was a lovely idea. He gave me your key and said he wouldn't breathe a word to you.'

Kate groaned inwardly. Oh, Dad, I *wish* you'd told me. I could have avoided all this! 'And so it is. For heaven's sake, stop looking so worried, Cathy. I'm thrilled! It's a marvellous party. Now come on, let's get another glass of champers before they down the lot.'

They were too late. All the champagne had gone, it was now a choice of beer, the hard stuff or wine. 'Are you acting as barman, Alex?'

'Yes m'lady!' Alex Peterson was half-smashed. 'What'll it be?'

'White wine.'

'White wine for the lady in white. Comin' up!'

And on it went. There were no complaints from the neighbours. Marilyn was no fool, she'd invited the neighbours to the party. Those who weren't already there arrived at different times as the evening wore on— some of them Kate didn't even know, except by sight. She had a couple more glasses of wine, laughed gaily when Kevin Dean grabbed her by the waist and started dancing with her, then she went in search of Marilyn.

'Well, Marilyn, you've excelled yourself.'

Marilyn looked like an angel, the way her light blonde hair was streaming around her shoulders. She was dancing with Roger in Kate's spare bedroom, as were several other couples. 'I came to congratulate you.'

'You're happy? You like it? You must be relieved to be having fun again, to be living again!'

Living again. Is that what this was? But what could she say? Marilyn meant well, all of them meant well. They would never begin to understand if she told them how she was really feeling, that she would rather be sitting quietly in an artist's studio, watching someone at work . . . No! She would not dwell on the impossible, she would not dwell on what couldn't be.

'Yes, Marilyn, very relieved.' She glanced at Roger. 'I'm glad you two have got together.'

Roger Dennison looked sheepish. He was dressed casually tonight, he had no tie on. He opened his mouth to say something, paused because he didn't know what to say, and before he needed to dream something up, Giles called to Kate from the doorway.

'Kate? There you are! Been looking for you. There's someone asking for you at the front door. I think we've got a gatecrasher.'

Kate doubted that very much. She walked unsteadily towards Giles. She'd had several glasses of wine by this time and it had finally started to take its toll. Her laughter was coming more easily and it was sounding less brittle, though it wasn't real. 'I doubt it. It's probably another of the neighbours.'

'No, it's not a neighbour. I asked.' Giles slipped an arm possessively around Kate's waist and walked her towards the front door. 'I think he's got himself mixed up, gone to the wrong party or something. This guy's dressed for dinner at Kensington Palace.'

'So what? So am I, thanks to you!' She swayed against him slightly and he caught her closer, looking puzzled as they reached the front door. It was closed. 'Perhaps he was a mirage. I left him standing here, right here.' Giles stabbed a finger in the direction of the floor. He flung the front door open as an after-thought.

And then the world stopped.

There were no voices in the flat, no people. There was no music, no Giles with his arm around her, no laughter.

There was only Adam.

He was standing in the corridor, arms folded across his massive chest. He was leaning lazily against the wall, looking breathtakingly attractive in a white, formal dinner jacket.

CHAPTER TEN

KATE stared and stared in disbelief. 'Adam!' That was all she could think of to say. Her heart was pounding at the sight of him. She was both hopeful and horrified. Why was he here? Here, when he was supposed to be in New York? And why was he looking at her like that?

'Good evening, Kate.' The open contempt on his face was just as plain in his voice. His eyes were moving from her to Giles and back again, noting the way Giles was holding her possessively against him.

Kate wrenched free of the photographer's grip. 'We were just . . .' She couldn't think, could hardly find her voice. The shock of seeing Adam had thrown her mind into a spin of confusion. Her attempt at an explanation only made things worse. 'Just having a party.'

'So I see.' Adam's angry eyes flicked back to Giles. 'Would you mind? I'd like a word with Kate, alone.'

'Yes, I'd mind.' Giles grinned, his attitude good-natured. 'Don't I know you from somewhere? Why don't you come in and have a drink, whoever you are!'

'Giles, please.' Kate turned to him anxiously. Her face had lost all its colour; it was this that made him do as she asked. 'Please leave us a moment.'

He shot a curious, suspicious look at Adam and nodded reluctantly. 'If you insist.' He laughed shortly, a sound of irritation, before planting a swift, unavoidable kiss on her mouth. 'But don't be long, Baby Doll. I'll be missing you.'

Kate pulled the door to and stepped into the corridor. She put her hands behind her back, placing them flat on the wall, leaning against them in an effort to stop them shaking. 'This—is certainly a surprise, Adam. I—I thought you were in New York.'

Adam hadn't moved. His eyes were as hard as flint as they travelled swiftly over her from the low neckline of the clinging white dress to the gold, high-heeled sandals on her feet. His tone was scathing. 'Baby Doll?'

'It's—just his pet name for me.' Wanting desperately to explain herself, she added lamely, 'These—some of my friends plotted a surprise party. You must think—I mean, I came out of the nursing home today, you see, and——'

'And you couldn't wait to show yourself off. Now you have your face and your freedom, you're making the most of it.' He took his eyes from her and glanced at the door to her apartment. 'It sounds more like an orgy. So this is your world, is it?'

'No! I mean, well, yes, but——'

'Goodbye, Kate.'

'*Adam!*' She almost screamed the word. He had started to walk away from her! He paused, turned around slowly. The look of disgust on his face made her want to die.

'Don't go, please! Come—come inside, have a drink. Let's talk——'

'Talk? I don't believe you and I have anything to say to each other. Besides, I think the man with the golden earring has plans for you. You'd better get back where you belong, back to the glitter and the glamour.'

His jibes cut into her painfully, he was giving her no time to explain things. 'Adam, please! Why—why are you here? If you have nothing to say, why did you come? And why are you dressed so formally?' And beautifully, she could have added. She would have been shocked on seeing him even if she'd been expecting him. In immaculate black trousers and tie, white jacket and shirt, he looked unrecognisable. Except that she knew every hair on his head. Except that she loved every familiar feature of his face. But Adam turned heads no matter what he was wearing. 'Why are you in London? Dolores told me you'd gone to New York.'

'So I did. I'm in London for twenty-four hours, that's all. Let's call it a case of unfortunate timing. I'm going back to my commitments in New York tomorrow.'

Tomorrow? The crazy, impossible hope she had felt on first seeing him died. She glanced at the door to her home, flinching as a sudden uproar of laughter filled her ears. The music was blaring now. Damn it! Damn them, all of them!

She turned back to see Adam disappearing round the corner at the end of the corridor. Panic-stricken, desperate, she ran after him. He was punching the button for the lift.

'Go back to your party,' he snapped. 'My curiosity's been more than satisfied.'

'What do you mean?' She wanted to reach out to him, to touch him, to beg him stay, to throw herself into his arms and tell him she loved him.

But she couldn't, wouldn't. Not in a million years. She had already behaved like a fool with him, staring and letting him see how affected she'd been by his appearance at her door. It would give him the laugh of his life if he knew how she really felt. It would also give him the greatest satisfaction to reject her when he had specifically warned her not to expect anything of him.

Before anything more could be said, Marilyn and Roger appeared. 'We're off.' Marilyn looked very pleased with herself.

Roger was looking at Adam. 'I say, aren't you A. E. de la Mare, the sculptor? I was at an exhibition of yours here in London last year. You are de la Mare, aren't you?'

Adam didn't even answer him. Marilyn cut in. 'It was a super party, Kate. But Roger and I have had enough.' She giggled. She was talking to Kate, she had her arm linked through Roger's, but her eyes were on Adam. 'It was fun, though, great fun! We must do it again soon, at my place. 'Night . . .'

Adam waited till the lift doors had closed. 'Roger?'

Kate nodded. The interruption had given her enough time in which to compose herself. She stood regally now, proudly, her attitude calm and collected. 'Roger Dennison. He's switched his affections.'

'So I gather. I thought he was in love with you.'

'So did he.'

'And that's the type you go for, is it? Hooray Henrys in Savile Row suits? They don't get much more *couth* than old Roger, do they? Which is more than can be said for your newest recruit, Giles. Giles makes quite a contrast!'

'Adam, you don't understand——'

'Oh, I understand, all right!' His eyes were blazing. 'I never knew you at all, did I, Kate? I only thought I did. It seems to me you go for all sorts of men,' he added, with a great deal of insinuation. 'You admire your admirers, no matter what their "type". Well, congratulations on the success of your operation, that's all I came to say. So goodbye, *Baby Doll*. Go on, get back to your party and Giles of the earring and the deeper shades of pink.'

'*Please!* It isn't like that——'

But he'd gone. He didn't wait for the lift, he took the stairs and walked away without another word.

Kate stayed where she was, she slumped against the wall and dropped her head in her hands. She didn't cry, she was too stunned even to do that. To think he had come to see her only to find her in the arms of a man, a man she didn't give a damn about! What must he be thinking of her now?

It was Cathy who came looking for her. 'Kate! What're you doing, standing there? Giles said you had a visitor——'

'I did. I——'

'You're as white as a sheet! What is it? Do you feel ill?'

'No, I—oh, Cathy! Adam was here and—and I hoped . . . But he wouldn't listen to me. He's gone away thinking——' She was dangerously close to tears now.

'What? And who is Adam?' Cathy slipped an arm around her shoulder.

'Adam de la Mare. He's—it doesn't matter.'

'The one you're in love with. This is the person you were pining for, crying over, isn't it?'

'Yes,' she admitted dully. 'And he couldn't care less about me.'

'Oh, Kate! I know how you're feeling, believe me. I've had my share of trouble with the opposite sex. Come on let's get you inside. You'd better rest, you're very pale and you're trembling.'

Kate held on to her arm, grateful for her level-headed presence. 'Cathy, would you—I mean, would you mind asking them all to go? They all know you were looking after me in the nursing home, they'll take it from you. You could tell them——'

'No problem,' Cathy said briskly. 'I'll explain that's it all getting a bit much, being your first day out of bed and all. I feel responsible, Kate. I should have kept out of it. I should have realised you wouldn't be up to a party tonight. You must be feeling weak after being so long in bed.'

She hadn't been feeling weak. She had felt fine, physically. Now she was weak, weak in the legs and weak in the heart. She felt as though a knife were wedged in her chest, it was hurting so much.

Getting rid of the gang was easier said than done. Kate shooed people out of her bedroom, the six who were dancing and the couple who were necking on the bed. She locked the door and lay down in the lamplight; her head was throbbing. Giles was the last to leave and he wouldn't go without a word with her.

'Kate?'

'Go away, I'm feeling like death.'

'Just a quick word, darling. Please.'

She got up. Giles hadn't done anything wrong, it wasn't his fault Adam had treated her the way he had. 'Well?'

'Who was he?'

'Who was whom?'

'Come off it, Kate! The big guy—you went white when you saw him. You've got it bad, haven't you?'

'Yes.' She sighed. What was the point in denying it? 'I've got it bad, Giles.'

He ran a finger down her nose and stooped to kiss the tip of it. 'Poor Baby. If you want someone to help you take your mind off him, you know where to reach me. Any time, any time at all, Kate. And for the record,' he added, smiling, 'I'm jealous as hell.'

When she heard the front door close after him, she emerged from her bedroom to find Cathy tidying up in the living-room. 'Oh, Lord! Just look at this lot!'

Chaos. It looked as if a bomb had dropped on the place. And there was a big burn mark on the white carpet. 'Leave it, Cathy. I don't care about the mess, I couldn't care less if they'd burnt the place down.'

Cathy was emptying ashtrays into a bin. 'I'll just take this out and then we'll have a cup of coffee.' She looked at Kate uncertainly. 'That is, if you don't mind? I thought—well, I thought you might like to talk.'

Kate was desperate to do just that and the nurse was someone she trusted. Unlike her friends, Cathy was a good listener; she cared, even though she'd known Kate only for a short time. She listened to the entire story without comment, her gentle green eyes widening in surprise, even shock, or laughing, frowning, as Kate told it all in minute detail.

'It seems to me,' she said at length, 'that Adam cared for you right from the start.'

Kate couldn't believe it. 'What? How do you make that out? He's a cruel, arrogant, insensitive, egotistical——'

'He's no such thing, and you know it. He treated you badly in the beginning for your own sake. If it hadn't been for him, you'd still be living like a hermit, still wrapped up in yourself and your problems—or what you imagined were your problems. I wish I'd met him,' she added with a smile. 'He sounds gorgeous in every way to me.'

Kate flopped back against the cushions of the settee. 'He is,' she admitted. 'He's everything I want in a man. I—heaven help me, I'm crazy about him! What am I going to do?'

The other girl was already thinking about that. It didn't seem hopeful, she had to admit. 'Except that he came here. I mean he did come to see you.'

'So what? I suppose he was curious, that's all, like everyone else. He came to take a look at me, to congratulate me, because he happened to be in the area.'

'In London, yes, not necessarily in the area. He did make something of an effort. It must have been almost midnight when he called.'

'What am I supposed to make of that? He didn't come to take me out!' She got to her feet, restless, angry with herself. 'When I think how I behaved with him tonight, I could curl up and die! I've got no pride, not where he's concerned, that's what he's reduced me to! How could I have chased after him like that, asking him to stay, letting him see how much I cared?'

But he hadn't seen that. Adam had seen what he wanted to see. In his mind she had switched from one lover to another—and he himself had been the man she'd amused herself with in between. She said all this to Cathy.

'I know, I know. It was unfortunate, his seeing you with Giles like that.'

'Giles! I wouldn't mind, but I don't even fancy him!' She broke off, looking around the room in dismay. 'It's all so pointless,' she said softly. 'Pointless.'

'What is?'

'Everything. The way I live. This world I'm in. My so-called friends. They wouldn't have rallied, you know, if things had turned out differently, if I were an ugly duckling. I wouldn't belong any more. But I'm still acceptable because I'm still beautiful,' she added bitterly. 'Big deal.'

'Kate, Kate, stop it. Look, you must get some sleep. I'll come back in the morning to help you clear up.'

'Aren't you working?'

'It's my day off tomorrow—today.' She looked at her watch. 'Great guns, it's almost four o'clock.'

'You could sleep here. There's a spare bed in there. Will you?'

'Of course. In fact I'd be grateful—I'm not tipsy but I did have too much to drink. I'm sure I'm over the legal limit.'

That settled it.

Kate got as far as the door and then turned, her attitude suddenly aggressive. 'We'll go out to lunch tomorrow. Then we can take a look round the shops if you're free. I'm damned if I'm going to break my heart over *him* any longer! I've got to forget him, I've *got* to!'

That was something else which was easier said than done. Late though it was, Kate couldn't get him out of her mind. Not that that was anything new. She got into bed, closed her eyes and saw him, looking magnificent, leaning against the wall in that lazy way of his, his brown eyes glittering with anger. If only she could think that was caused by jealousy! But he had looked at her with contempt. He had said he didn't know her, after all. That he only thought he had.

But why had he come visiting so late? Midnight was hardly the time to drop in on someone. Had he made a special effort to see her while he was in London? At some time, any time, during his few hours here? Or had she been an afterthought, someone he could get a cup of coffee from after being somewhere else? Where had he been that he was dressed so uncharacteristically?

All her questions were answered the following evening, when she finally got round to looking at her newspaper. She'd spent the day with Cathy Mansfield and had walked miles, window shopping.

It was almost six in the evening when she put her feet up and had a look at the paper. There was no mystery. She had been an afterthought as far as Adam was concerned.

He was mentioned in the arts section in the paper, though the article was not primarily about him. It began:

London's Grosvenor House Hotel was the venue last night for the 80th birthday celebration of Samuel J. S. Gray, England's most eminent portrait painter, whose work can be seen in no fewer than nine of Britain's stately homes and several Royal palaces at home and abroad.

In attendance at the party, which was described by its organiser as an 'intimate' affair for 'a few friends' (some hundred guests), were members of the Royal Academy who included Helen Atherley, whose seascape paintings are familiar to us all, and A. E. de la Mare, the sculptor. Mr de la Mare, who emerges only 'when necessary' from the homes at which he also works (he has a villa in Tuscany, Italy, and a house in his native Guernsey, in the Channel Islands), interrupted a stay in New York to attend last night's party. Always reluctant to talk to the press, whom he openly regards as a 'necessary evil'(!), Mr de la Mare was untypically forthcoming last night. 'This is more than a celebration for an octogenarian,' he told us, 'Samuel J. S. Grey has been my friend for many years. Friend, one-time mentor and an unceasing source of inspiration and admiration. His energy, creative and otherwise, is phenomenal. It is a privilege to be here with him on this occasion.'

A. E. de la Mare had crossed the Atlantic after attending the preview of an exhibition of his work at the Bernstein Gallery in Manhattan. He is returning to New York tomorrow—where he will lecture to the sculptors of tomorrow. 'The sharing, the passing on of knowledge,' he said, 'is one's duty.'

That is as may be. But talent cannot be taught, as he must surely know. If the talent of the likes of A. E. de la Mare could be passed on in classes, the world of art would be very much the richer.

The guest of honour at last night's party said . . .

There was no more about Adam. Kate put the paper down. So that was it. He was back in New York now. She got tiredly to her feet and headed for the bathroom, turned on the taps and sat on the edge of the bath while it filled. Work, that's what she must do now. Get down to some hard work. There would be no more parties, no more attempts to escape from her thoughts and feelings with such desperate means. Rather, she would work as she had never worked before.

She stripped off and got into the bath, wishing the hot water could ease her aching heart as easily as it eased her tired feet.

CHAPTER ELEVEN

'HERE you are, here's mud in your eye!' Cathy filled two wine glasses and handed one to Kate. 'How's it going? You look a bit done in. What were you doing today?'

'Working on the ad.' Kate kicked off her shoes and put her feet up. They were in the small flat Cathy shared with another nurse, in Kilburn.

It was five weeks since she'd left the nursing home and in that time she and Cathy had become firm friends, spending the evening together about twice a week. Kate looked forward to those evenings. They would go out for a meal or perhaps to the pictures or they'd stay at home and get a take-away, watch TV or natter. Simple things. Kate was more than happy to have dropped out of her old, nightly social circle with their 'Darling!' here and 'Darling!' there. More than content to pull on a pair of jeans and a blouse after work, not to have to maintain the image she had during the day. Of course, during the day she was mixing with people she knew, photographers and other models. But there was nothing she could do about that. She was working like a demon, taking on as much as she could get.

Her friends were baffled by the change in her, most especially Marilyn. 'What's with you?' she'd demanded more than once. 'Why won't you come out any more? Why are you working so hard—saving up for something, are you?' That had been a joke, supposedly. Kate was earning a lot of money but she wasn't spending it, not because she was saving up but because she didn't buy the vast amount of clothes she used to go through, clothes she wore only a few times before they were discarded. She didn't need to; she didn't have to worry about being seen in the same things now, she wasn't going out on dates or to parties and so on.

Adam was constantly on her mind, and in her heart. Hence the hard work, the seeking of something else to occupy her thoughts. It didn't help much, though. She had been to Bristol twice, to spend a weekend with her parents, but it hadn't been much of a break. Nothing helped, really, and every week she waited impatiently, foolishly, for the arrival of a letter from Aunt Dolly. Kate wrote to her regularly, cheerfully, telling her of the work she'd been doing, never mentioning Adam except to say 'Give my regards . . .' at the end of each letter. The thought was never reciprocated; he was still in Guernsey but there was never a word, never a message from him via his stepmother's letters to Kate.

'I'd better have an early night. You must throw me out soon.' She raised her glass to Cathy and sighed before taking a drink. 'Models aren't paid to look done in. Working under those hot studio lights doesn't help.' And the weather was impossibly hot, too. It was the end of July and it had been scorching for the past few weeks. She felt limp and wrung-out, physically as well as emotionally. She wished she lived in the country, she wanted to get out of the dusty city. London had once been enchanting, exciting to her, but not any more.

'Tell me something.' Cathy was grinning, making an effort to distract her. She had seen the look in Kate's eyes and she knew who was in her mind. As usual. 'This new shampoo you're advertising, is it any good?'

Kate laughed. 'I don't know, I've only tried it once and I wasn't happy with the result. I prefer my old one.'

'Charming! How can you say complimentary things about it and recommend it when you don't even use it?'

'I don't, the man in the voice-over does that. I just stand there twirling my head and smiling.' She looked heavenward. 'But I take your point. This is a funny kind of job. I'm getting rapidly sick of it.'

It was hard work, too. Cathy had come to realise
that. She had always, like lots of other people, assumed
that the work of a model was a piece of cake. You
didn't have to *do* much. But you did; it was wearing,
dashing from place to place to do a fashion show,
rehearsing, doing rapid changes of clothes, or working
in a studio, standing around waiting while cameras were
set up, having to look one's best all the time, vivacious
and smiling and happy. Or business-like. Or sophisticated or sexy or both—whatever the 'look' was for the
particular occasion. 'Kate, have you given any thought
to the idea of taking a holiday?'

'I don't want to.' She smiled to soften her words.
Cathy had booked a holiday in Spain long since, with
Greta, her flat-mate, and both girls had asked Kate if
she'd like to go with them. They were going next
month, for the last two weeks of August.

'But there's no problem. I asked the travel agent, he
can't book you on the same flight as us, you'd have to
leave from Gatwick the day after, but he can get you in
the same hotel.'

'Really, Cathy, the answer's no. It's sweet of you, and
Greta. I appreciate it but I'm just not in the mood for a
holiday.'

'You're not just referring to your commitments.'

'No, I could get out of those. Modelling is very much
a rat-race, you know. There's always someone new
waiting to step in. I'd be lousy company. Besides,
three's an awkward number for girls on holiday, I
always think.'

'But——'

'No, thanks just the same. Don't forget I had three
months off, I'm not exactly in need of a rest!'

'You could have fooled me,' said Cathy, sighing.

During early August, Marcia Holman put her foot
down with Kate. Marcia had been running the model

agency for ten years and she planned on giving a party on the premises, to celebrate. 'It's on the twenty-sixth, after we close shop. Around seven o'clock. I want you to be there, Kate, and I will not take no for an answer, nor do I want to hear any lame excuses about your staying in to paint your toenails that night.'

Kate laughed at the older woman's aggression. 'There's no need to attack me like that, of course I'll be there. I wouldn't want to miss your celebration, Marcia.'

'Oh.' There wasn't much Marcia could say in the face of such a gracious acceptance. 'Oh, well that's all right, then. Sorry to jump on you like that but I do know you've been acting oddly, spending all your nights at home, never going out. Marilyn's told me.'

'Marilyn among others, I've no doubt. Is there any coffee going?' Kate sat down, pulled off her shoes and put her feet up on Marcia's coffee table. She had come into the agency to collect a cheque, not to be read the riot act. 'Anyhow, you're wrong, they're wrong. I do go out. With my friend, Cathy.' She didn't add, 'When she isn't on night-duty or when I'm not feeling so damned blue I can't face anyone at all, even Cathy.'

'Cathy? Cathy who?'

'Mansfield. You met her the night I got out of the nursing home, at the party in my flat.'

Ouch! Kate looked down at the floor. Of all the time she had spent with Adam, all the memories she had, she tried to forget that particular one. 'Besides, how can you think I spend "all" my evenings at home when you yourself provide me with work for some of them? What about those fashion shows at the Dorchester last week, I was out then, wasn't I?'

'Yes.' Marcia shot her a hard look. 'And you refused to have dinner with Max Simmonds! He went to see what sort of shows this agency is capable of——'

'And to weigh up your models.'

'Of course,' Marcia accepted that as read. 'He's a dress-designer, what do you expect? He could put a lot of business our way and you wouldn't even have a meal with him! Are you nuts?'

Kate didn't spare Marcia the truth. Why should she? There was a misunderstanding here and it ought to be put right. 'I'm a model, Marcia, one of the best in the country. I am not a prostitute.'

'What the hell is that supposed to mean? I wasn't for one second suggesting——'

Hastily, Kate held up both hands. 'No, no, I know that. For heaven's sake! It's just that Max Simmonds said something filthy to me. I think he's warped. Without any encouragement whatever, he told me in no uncertain terms what he'd like to do to me. And it didn't sound normal to me. I'd disliked him on sight and he had much more than dinner on his mind.'

'Christ!'

'Quite so.'

Marcia was apologising again. 'I'm sorry, Kate, I had no idea . . .'

'That's okay,' she answered tiredly. Marcia had had no way of knowing. 'I'll be off. I'm longing for a soak in the bath.'

'Don't forget your cheque.'

'Thanks. I had.'

'How's the new car?'

'A car is a car is a car. I'll see you.'

Kate left the premises and strolled through the West End to the parking space she had found by sheer fluke. She didn't normally drive into the heart of London but she'd been out of town on an assignment today and it hadn't seemed worthwhile, switching to the tube to get into the centre of the metropolis. Her new car was nothing special, just a newer version of her previous one, a small saloon.

She got home to find a letter from Aunt Dolly on her

doormat. Against her better judgment she tore it open with an eagerness which was pitiful. There was never a word from Adam, nor would there be this time.

There wasn't.

But there was some news about him. Aunt Dolly's letter started with it. '... Adam has gone back to Tuscany, so I won't see him until next year. I don't understand it, really. He normally stays on Guernsey until September. It can't be that he's missing Elena because he'd have brought her over for a holiday or he'd have gone to visit her. He's still in a strange mood, Kate, nothing's changed in all these weeks. I'm wondering if it's *you* he's missing? I'd like to think so. It can't be a coincidence, the way he changed while you were here. Just as you changed. Are you aware of that? You blossomed after you made friends with Adam, I saw it happening to you. I was thrilled at the time, but—well, dear, I can't help wondering what happened. What went wrong? Adam never mentioned your name to me after you left here and if I spoke of you, he merely grunted and changed the subject. Either that, or he got angry. Neither of you have talked to me. Is there anything to tell? Is there anything I can do to help you, both of you? Either of you? Or am I imagining things? Perhaps I'm being an interfering old woman who should mind her own business ...'

Kate screwed the letter up and clenched it in her fist, her hand at her mouth. She closed her eyes tightly, thinking aloud. 'Oh, Aunt Dolly! How sweet you are! There's nothing, *nothing* to tell. I'm deeply in love with your own dear stepson, but I can't let you know that. He must never know, and much as I love you, I couldn't trust you not to tell him. He despises me, he thinks I'm some sort of play-girl and he scorns my life-style, or what he thinks is my life-style.'

She put pen to paper immediately. After several abortive attempts at a reply, she gave up and cooked herself an omelette. There was no hurry. Besides, she simply couldn't work out what to say. There was no way she was going to tell Dolores the truth, nor did she want to hurt her feelings by ignoring the subject of Adam altogether. Her aunt's letter was full of it, it had to be answered somehow.

At a little after midnight, after more attempts which had been rejected, Kate read through her latest effort and decided to send it. She hoped it would sound natural. It was a chatty letter, written on two sheets, full of news about what she'd been doing, about the stifling August weather and how it made work seem harder, how everyone was wishing for a storm so it might cool down for a bit. Only after this did she mention Adam, in as casual a way as she could, 'About Adam, by the way, I think you're worrying too much. If he is still moody, it's probably because he's taken too much on. As for him and me, there's nothing I can tell you except that he and I are very different people. Worlds apart. Surely you realise that. Oh, we had a lot of fun together but it was just a sort of holiday thing basically, I suppose. Underlying it all there was—I don't know what to call it—a fundamental difference in us I can only call a personality clash.'

It would do nicely. Kate was pleased with the effort, she had managed not to tell any lies. She started a final paragraph with, 'Did I tell you I took delivery of my new car last week . . .'

The next morning, she read it through and decided definitely to post it.

Another week rolled by. The next letter Kate had from Dolores was a hurriedly written one and it reminded her of her aunt's occasional bouts of eccentricity. She hadn't mentioned to Kate that she was going away on holiday with some members of the bridge club, she just assumed she knew! And there was no mention at all of Adam. 'I'm in the throes of packing,' it said, 'so I can't write much but I'll send you a postcard. I hate leaving the dogs but they'll be well looked after, I know. Mrs Sarre can't have them because as you know she already has three of her own and two boys so I'm putting them in kennels. I mean, oh, well, I think you know what I mean! It does read oddly, doesn't it? But she's going to look after the goats for me. And my cat. And my plants. It's just as well I have no other pets, isn't it?'

Kate read the letter with relief, and laughter. She closed her eyes and could see clearly her aunt's cosy living-room with its touch of orderly chaos. She put the letter away in the drawer where all her aunt's letters were kept, and left for work.

The weather broke in the middle of the month. There were several storms, violent ones, and afterwards it began to get cooler by the day. Cathy was on holiday. She had gone to Spain just as the weather changed. Nice timing. Kate got a postcard from her in which she said she'd met this wonderful man . . .

Were there any?

'Kate, you really are becoming cynical.' She spoke to her reflection in the bathroom mirror. 'As Adam once told you. Just because you can't have the man you want, just because—and you're talking to yourself. Again. You've been spending too much time alone.'

She had, too. Oddly enough, there had been no work for three consecutive days. It happened like that sometimes. She had spent the time cleaning her flat from top to bottom, keeping herself busy. Keeping her hands busy, at any rate. Her mind had been elsewhere while she'd worked, thinking of pleasanter sights than her flat, imagining herself high in the sky in a private plane, peering down on Guernsey. Or sailing over to Herm. Or climbing over the rocks on the beach. Or looking delightedly at the mass of bluebells on the walk down to the sands at Fermain Bay. Adam had taken her there especially to see the bluebells, knowing how much she loved flowers.

During the last week of August, it started getting warm again and everyone who had previously complained about the heat started hoping for an Indian summer. There was no pleasing the British where the weather was concerned. Including herself.

On the day of Marcia's party at the agency, it was drizzling. It was that fine sort of rain in which one seems to get wetter than in a downpour. Kate stood by her living-room window, looking out and wondering what to wear. She didn't want to go the party but she had to, she couldn't let Marcia down. Or could she? Surely she wouldn't be missed among a crowd?

'I'd better go.' After taking a shower, she did her face and looked through her wardrobe without enthusiasm. Though she hadn't bought any new clothes of late there was still plenty of choice. But she had no enthusiasm for anything, the clothes, the party or anything else. It was all too much of an effort.

When the phone rang, she glanced at her watch, wondering who it could be. It was six o'clock. She got very few phone calls other than those relating to work these days. Cathy was away, so it had to be one of her parents. She picked up the receiver, her voice desultory. 'Hello?'

'Hello, Kate.'

'Who is this?' she demanded. It was a joke, it must be! Her legs turned to water and she lowered herself on to a chair. All sorts of things flashed through her mind. It was Giles. It was Roger. But she knew the voice belonged to neither of them. It was the most distinctive of voices, one she had heard speaking to her every day for the past two months. In her head.

It was Adam.

CHAPTER TWELVE

WHEN she could find her voice, she said, 'What do you want?' It came out as a whisper. 'Why—are you ringing? Where are you?'

The gravelly voice was perfectly controlled, as casual as if this call were an everyday occurrence. 'I'm in London for the night. I got in at Gatwick an hour ago. I thought we'd have dinner together.'

Kate closed her eyes, struggling for composure, trying to breathe properly. She was joyous to the point of feeling faint. And yet, because of it, she was angry with herself. And with him. How dare he phone her? How dare he disturb her like this when she'd been fighting so hard to get over him, to forget him? How dare he ring her out of the blue and expect her to drop everything to go out with him!

Drop everything? What was there to drop? But he didn't need to know that. 'I'm sorry,' she managed, 'I have a ...' She had been going to say 'date' but that would sound as though she were going out with a man. 'A date.' She said it after all. Why shouldn't she be going out with a man?

'Then you'll ring him and cancel. You're coming out with me tonight.'

No! No, he wasn't going to take control of her like that. He *wasn't*. Not ever again. 'I'm afraid I can't do that,' she said coolly. 'It isn't that sort of date, actually.' She went on quickly but calmly. 'The woman who runs the modelling agency is celebrating its tenth anniversary with a party. It's starting in an hour and I'm obliged to be there.'

He had the audacity to laugh at that. 'Obliged? Come

on, Kate, you can do better than that with your silly lies! Why don't you just say you don't want to see me?'

She couldn't. Dear God, she wanted to see him more than anything else in the world. If he only knew how much! Her fingers were clenching the telephone receiver so tightly, her knuckles were white. Her mind was racing, wondering what to say. She felt torn. She daren't see him, she just daren't, she couldn't trust herself. It would be all too easy to start blabbering and telling him how she really felt. But telling him she didn't want to see him was impossible, more than she could bring herself to say. 'Don't be silly. Why should I want to avoid you? But there it is, I'm committed for the evening, it's as simple at that.' She was racing now, giving him no chance to interrupt because she knew only too well the power he had over her. He had always been able to get his own way with her, one way or another. Given the state she was in these days, it was all too dangerous keeping up this conversation. 'Ring me the next time you're in town, if you must insist on maintaining this pointless contact with me. Goodbye, Adam.'

She slammed the phone down, hoping he got the message, terrified in case he phoned back. And terrified in case he didn't.

He didn't.

Like the fool that she was, she sat by the telephone, willing it to ring again. At length she could wait no longer. It was six-forty and she had to get to the agency. Suddenly she wanted to go, not to the party especially; she just wanted to get out. Flinging on the first dress she put her hand on, she quickly brushed her hair, picked up her wrap and headed for her car. Having second thoughts, she walked on to the main road and hailed a taxi. She wouldn't drive tonight.

She was going to get drunk tonight.

Once inside the taxi, she vowed she would do just

that. She would have to do something to numb her mind, to forget that phone call, to get the sound of Adam's voice out of her head for at least a few hours.

'Kate, darling, you look *gorgeous*!' Marilyn was there, with Roger. They were all there, the usual gaggle of girls and their boyfriends.

'So do you,' she said honestly. Marilyn always looked gorgeous. 'Hello, Roger. Oh, excuse me, there's Marcia—must go and congratulate her on the occasion.' She made her way to Marcia and her husband and handed them the gift she'd brought. 'Here's to your next ten years, Marcia.'

'Hear, hear!' Philip Holman, who was in business for himself and had nothing to do with the running of the agency, raised his glass in a toast. 'To Marcia—my hard-working, lovely and enterprising wife!'

Marcia laughed at that. 'How many drinks have you had, Philip? To my beautiful girls!' she amended. 'Where would I be without them?'

Thankfully there was no music; it wasn't that sort of party. People were circulating, chatting, drinking cocktails. Kate found it impossibly boring and at eight o'clock she glanced at her watch and considered leaving; she had put in an appearance, had done her duty. But what then? What of the rest of the evening? She simply couldn't face going home to that empty flat again. Not tonight. And Cathy wasn't around to turn to. Better to be here with this lot than moping at home. She went in search of another drink.

Philip Holman was searching for her. 'Kate, there's someone asking for you. You might have told me you'd invited Adam de la Mare to our modest little shindig! Does Marcia know? She'll be delighted——'

Kate had stopped listening. Adam was walking towards her, his stride long and purposeful. Dressed in denims, shirt and jeans, he looked incongruous among the others at this 'modest little shindig'. He towered

over all of them and, to Kate, he looked beautiful.
Shocked to the core, she lost the power of speech. Her
mouth went dry and her throat seemed to close. With a
smile in Adam's direction Philip drifted away, leaving
her to cope alone.

'Good evening, Kate.' Adam's voice, his face, was
impassive. There was no smile, no anger, nothing. 'I'm
not used to having people hang up on me. I wanted to
talk to you.'

'Go away.' It was little more than a croak. She felt as
though her heart would burst, she loved him so. She
had ached for so long to see him, she could hardly bear
to look at him. Just looking at him, just—just being
with him gave her more happiness than she could
handle. All composure had deserted her; she was scared
of whatever was coming next.

'I've no intention of doing that. I told you, I want to
talk to you. In private.' He glanced round the room, a
hint of irritation showing now. 'My God! Come on,
let's get out of this babble.'

'I'm not going anywhere.' Kate held on to the back
of a chair as if to prove it. 'I have to stay.'

She had said the last few words almost desperately
but Adam was unmoved. In a manner which brought
back a flood of memories, his big hand clamped down
on her shoulder and he told her, very quietly, that they
were leaving this minute. 'You've done your bit.
Besides, this is a cocktail party and it'll break up
shortly. We can have dinner, after all.'

If she argued, there would be a very embarrassing
scene. She knew that without a doubt. Once Adam
made up his mind on something, he was immovable. If
she defied him he'd simply pick her up bodily and carry
her out. And that would give them all something to talk
about! 'All right, all right. Let go of me, I've got to get
my wrap and say good night to Marcia . . .'

Firstly she escaped into the loo. Other girls were in

there, including Marilyn, who didn't miss a thing, especially where attractive men were concerned. 'So you're letting us have another look at him, eh? How about introducing me this time? I noticed you didn't bother that night at your place. You've been keeping him to yourself!'

'Can you blame her?' Elizabeth Stanley put in her opinion. 'I saw him come in just now.' She grinned. 'Mm-mm! Talk about big! He's just my type! Who is he, Kate? He doesn't look like your type, come to think of it.'

Marilyn answered for her. 'He's Adam de la Mare, a Guernseyman. He's a sculptor. I'd never heard of him, but Roger knows a bit about him, he's got some of his work, and his father's got several pieces.' She turned back to Kate. 'He's quite a catch. No wonder you stayed so long on Guernsey!' She gave Kate her prettiest wink. 'What a dark horse you are, we've all been thinking you unsociable of late but you've been seeing him, haven't you? No wonder you haven't been available! All this time and you never said a word!'

Kate answered with a tight little smile and a rapid, 'Good night.' She hadn't known what to say. She felt sick with nervousness. If she couldn't cope with the girls talking about him, how was she going to cope with the man himself?

She opened the door to the ladies' room to find Adam waiting right outside. Marcia was talking to him. On a first-name basis. 'Are you sure you won't stay for a drink, Adam? You're more than welcome. I'd like——'

'No. Thank you, Mrs Holman, but Kate and I have things to talk about.'

His hand was already under Kate's elbow, propelling her towards the door. She looked helplessly, apologetically, over her shoulder and caught Marcia's look. The other woman was rolling her eyes dramatically,

grinning, giving a thumbs-up sign. Kate groaned
inwardly, wondering what on earth she was presuming
from all this.

Adam steered her on to the street, saying nothing
until they were well clear of the agency. It was still
drizzling with rain. 'I've got a hire car. It's just round
the corner.'

'How did you find me? How did you know which
agency I work for? I never mentioned——'

'It wasn't difficult, haven't you heard of the Yellow
Pages? Holman's was the only agency where someone
answered the phone. Get in, Kate. We'll go back to
your flat first so you can . . . dress down a bit.'

She got in the car, closing her eyes against his jibe.
He was right, she was over-dressed, even for a cocktail
party. The garment she had happened to put her hands
on was black and silver, a shimmery little number she'd
bought last year but never worn. When he got behind
the wheel, she said, 'I'm not going out with you, Adam.
Please drop me at home and then leave me. Leave
me——' She broke off. Tears were stinging behind her
eyes and she was too exhausted to have a scene with
him. Wearily, she finished the sentence. 'Leave me
alone. For good.'

Ten minutes passed before Adam spoke again. He
waited until they'd reached her flat, brought the car to a
halt. The short drive had been agony for Kate. She'd
kept her face averted all the time, certain that if she
looked at him, she'd make a complete fool of herself.

When he switched the engine off, he caught hold of
her roughly, forcing her to face him. 'What's the
matter? Am I too dull for you, is that it? You'd
rather be with Giles or whoever's the latest man in
your life?'

Very quietly she said, 'There is no man in my life.'

'Tell it to the Marines, Kate.' He leaned over and
opened the passenger door, his body brushing against

hers, the back of his arm touching her breasts. The contact made her gasp and it did not go unheard.

'Me, too.' Adam fixed her with his steady brown gaze. It was still light and in his eyes she could almost see what he was thinking. It was as if he were battling with himself, resenting what he was about to say. 'I don't even have to touch you to feel the effect you have on me. All I have to do is think of you. I don't care how many men you've had——'

'Adam!' She gasped again. Oh, if only he knew! What *did* he think of her, what did he think she *was*?

'I don't care,' he persisted, 'you still want me. Physically, at least.' He pulled away from her, his big hands clenching the steering wheel now. 'That's one thing we have in common, isn't it, Kate? And it will have to do. I can only hope that it's enough.'

'Enough?' Inwardly, she started trembling. 'What are you talking about?'

'Marriage.' He spat the word out as though he hated the very sound of it. 'I want you. And it looks as if that's the only way I'm going to get you. To get some *peace*!' There was another, distasteful, twist of his mouth. 'I'm here to ask you to marry me.'

Kate didn't even bother to answer that. She got out of the car and ran.

CHAPTER THIRTEEN

SHE ran blindly, taking the stairs to her flat two at a time, stumbling and forcing herself forward again. As she reached her door she was nearly hysterical, fumbling in her bag for her key.

Familiar fingers closed around her wrist. 'Allow me.'

'Get away from me!' She hit out at him, her evening bag and its few contents scattering on the floor.

Adam calmly picked them up, opened the door and literally pushed her inside.

'Stop that! How *dare* you! Get *out* of here, I've got nothing to say to you.' She was crying now, noisily, helplessly, and she immediately contradicted herself. 'What sort of sick joke was that? How could you think for one minute I'd even consider marrying you? You must be off your head if you think, if you think . . .'

Covering her face with her hands, she stood in the hall, crying like a frightened little girl, not daring to look in case he'd gone, not daring to look in case he hadn't. Her mascara had run, tears were streaming down her face and her shoulders were shaking. In other words she did that which she had always feared she might do: she made a complete and utter fool of herself.

It was too much for her, the way his arms came gently around her, the way his lips brushed against her hair. 'What, Kate? If I think what?'

'If——' She hiccupped. 'If you think I'd marry you.'

Adam closed his eyes and said a silent prayer of thanks. Relief flooded through him. She was his. He knew it now. He knew it without a doubt. She loved him. Why this was so, how it could be, he didn't know, he was only grateful for it. But he was also afraid. For

her, for himself, for the future. 'Why?' he asked softly.
'Why won't you consider marrying me?'

It was no good, she couldn't pretend any more, not
any more. It was too much, being held by him like this.
'Because I love you,' she said miserably, almost
collapsing against him. 'And yes, I want you. I want
you desperately. As much as you want me. But you're
not going to have me. You'll never have me, Adam. I
would never marry a man who doesn't love me, and
much as I want you, I couldn't handle an affair with
you. Not now. It's far too late for that sort of thing. It
would destroy me. I love you too much.' Her face was
against his chest, against the bare skin where his shirt
was open at the neck. She could feel his chin resting
lightly on the top of her head and she waited for the
rumble of his laughter.

There was no laughter. Instead she felt his arms close
more tightly around her, felt him breathing out slowly.
She felt his mouth move over the black silk of her hair
until he was speaking softly against her ear. 'Thank
God for that! Because I love you too, Kate. I've loved
you since the day I met you.'

She tried to pull away from him but he wouldn't
allow it. He held her in the circle of his arms, looking
down at her. 'I mean it.'

He was holding her loosely now but she was
struggling to breathe, even so. 'You—I don't believe
that! You can't mean it.'

Adam let go of her but he caught hold of her hand
quickly lest she try to run away again. Never, he was
never going to let her run from him again. He moved in
the direction of the living-room, made her sit by his
side. He lifted her hand to his mouth and kissed the
palm, his lips trailing to the tips of her fingers, kissing
them one by one. 'I always mean what I say, you know
that.' He stopped what he was doing to look at her, his
eyes filled with pain. 'I was in love once before. Just

once. I was engaged to . . . she died, Kate. She and I—
we were both twenty-one and——'

'I know.' Unable to bear the look in his eyes, she
clung tightly to his hand. 'Aunt Dolly told me. It—
helped me to understand.'

'Understand?'

'You. Why you'd locked up your heart. I—thought
that's what you'd done. But perhaps that was a way of
easing my battered ego, my wounds. I had to find some
explanation, some consolation, because you didn't love
me. Because of it, because I thought you could never
love me, I assumed you were still in love with Margaret.
How's that for vanity?'

'Margaret was fifteen years ago. No, I got over her
death a long time ago, years ago. At least, I did in one
way. At first I vowed I'd never love again. An
understandable reaction. Intellectually I knew it was
improbable. Yet I never did—until you. I suppose a
part of me went on resisting, an emotional part which
had nothing to do with reality. That part of me was
afraid of loving and losing again. Even with you, I tried
to tell myself I merely felt sorry for you, those first few
days, seeing you trying to hide your face, such a
gorgeous woman and so lacking confidence, thinking
your life was over. I knew what was in your mind. I'd
gone through a similar hopelessness after Margaret's
death. I understood and I was very moved, and I tried
to convince myself I only felt sorry for you. But it was
more than that. Right from the start, I knew I had to
help you. I loved you then, Kate. I *cared*, I cared
enough to be cruel—to be kind.'

She smiled, a faint, sad sort of smile, thinking of
Cathy. Yes, he had cared, he still did—but he didn't
love her. It couldn't be true . . . 'Someone else has
pointed that out to me.'

Adam's expression changed, hardened. 'Who've you
been talking to about me? One of your——'

'A girlfriend, only a girlfriend.' Panic took hold. 'Adam, you've got to listen to me, you've got to believe me! There is no man in my life. How could there be when I've spent every minute of every day wanting you? I can't bear what you're thinking—what you think of me.'

'What I think of you? Kate, I *love* you! Nothing else matters.'

But it did, it mattered very much. 'No! I don't believe that.'

He misunderstood her protest. 'You'd better, you will,' he said roughly, catching hold of her, 'because I intend to spend every day of my life proving it to you! Look at me, look at me, Kate. Now tell me you don't believe it.'

She looked at him, she listened to that which his eyes were telling her. It was true, it was the truth! And in a way, it was more than she could ever have wished for. He loved her—no matter what. She got up, moved away from him in an effort to think more detachedly. 'Why did you warn me off? If you really loved me, why did you treat me so badly? Why did you blow hot and cold like that, snapping and——'

'Don't.' Adam shook his head, wanting to rid himself of the memories. 'I've never forgiven myself for all that. Kate, I—it's hard to explain. You see, I had no idea how you felt. No, really. Don't look at me like that, I mean it. When I said—when I *accused* you of falling in love, I was transferring to you my own feelings. Don't you see? I was kidding myself. My darling, you've got to believe me. It wasn't you I was warning off, it was *myself*. It was the part of me which didn't want to love. And lose. I never thought you could be mine, we're so different, the way we run our lives is different, I never dreamt you could fall for me. I was trying constantly to resist you, to keep away but—for most of the time, I couldn't. And then I'd get angry with myself, with you,

because you had such a hold over me. I thought i
hopeless. Not only am I considerably older than you,
was convinced you must think me boring.'

'*Boring?*' There was nothing she could do but laugh
'Boring!' She ran over to him, she knelt by his side an
flung her arms round him. 'You *idiot!*'

'You see what I mean? You might love me but yo
don't think very highly of me, do you?' He caught hol
of her, lifting her back to the settee, reaching for her
laughing.

Kate kept her distance. She wasn't laughing an
more. 'Adam, it's your turn to listen——'

'Just a minute.' His amusement disappeared. 'Yo
haven't given me your answer. I proposed to you
remember? I've been afraid, Kate, I still am. My life
style and yours, I don't know how we can satisfy bot
our needs, but I'm more than willing to try. I'll mak
you happy, I swear it. I'll meet you more than halfway
darling. We'll take holidays often, we'll have fun, I'
mix with people more, as much as I can stand to
I'm——'

'No, you won't.' Silent tears trickled from her eyes
In those few moments, all the love she felt for hin
welled up and overflowed, it could not be contained an
longer. Yes, he loved her, how he loved her! 'Hold me
Adam, just hold me tight and listen while I tell yo
what I'm really about these days.'

He listened, finally. He held her close and he listene
and from time to time, he kissed her. She told hin
everything, of her disillusionment with the people sh
mixed with, worked with, of her new and different wa
of thinking, of her disillusionment with her life-style
what used to be her life-style, of how she longed to liv
in the country, to have a quiet life, of her new values
'Whether it was living in Guernsey or whether it wa
you, or a mixture of both, I'm not sure. All I know i
that I came back to London a very, very differen

person. With different needs, different wants. All of which were embodied in you, my love for you and the life I could only dream of sharing with you. Adam . . .' At that point, her voice faded because it hurt to think back. 'You'll never know how I felt, the night you came here, the night of that awful party. Marilyn had organised it and she meant well, everyone meant well. It was just their way of going about things. But I hated every minute of it. Yet, in a way I felt trapped. I—was playing a part, but not to the extent you imagine. Roger Dennison never meant anything to me, neither did Giles. Would you believe I've never even been out with the man?'

'If you say so, of course I believe it. Oh, Kate!' He caught hold of her, crushing her painfully against him. She didn't protest, she revelled in the security of it. When I think—I could have murdered you that night, you and him! I was mad with jealousy, I went away and called myself every kind of cretin. I'd come then to ask you to marry me. I didn't hold out any hope, but I had to ask. I was acting on my own advice about the necessity of taking risks in life. I had to try. One always has hope. I've been unable to function without you. I couldn't work properly, I couldn't sleep, I—nothing has inspired me, nothing has been able to touch me, move me, except thoughts of you. I've tried to work on other things but every time I went in to my studio, I was obsessed with the idea of you, you! So I've started work on my life-size model of you.'

'And?'

'And it's going to be the most beautiful thing I've ever created. But it won't be half as beautiful as the real thing.' Adam paused, the smile fading from his eyes. 'I love you, Kate. I'm obsessed with you and I'm very happy to be in that state—now.'

She smiled. She knew all about being obsessed, just as she knew about the pain it could cause, what he'd

been through, the sleepless nights . . . 'I know, darling, I
know. How about a drink? I need one, will you do the
honours?'

Adam crossed to the bar, took two glasses down
from the mirrored shelves. Only then did he seem to
notice his surroundings. He took a good look around
the living room. 'Good grief,' he said, slowly, as if
bemused. 'This is one bloody awful room, Kate.'

'I know that, too.' She was laughing.

'It's so colourless . . .'

'Yes, darling.'

'And there's nothing of you in here. It has no—no
personality, no *feeling*.'

Kate knew all about that, as well. 'It doesn't belong to
me,' she said, 'it belongs to someone else, another girl.'

Adam smiled at that. 'Maybe you'll introduce me
some time? Is she a looker? If so, I might switch my
affections because you, Miss Sumner, look a mess.
Your gorgeous blue eyes are pink right now and you've
got black circles under them. You offend the artist in
me,' he added dramatically, putting fingers to his
forehead.

'Get you!' Kate laughed and added something
unladylike and rude. God, she was happy! This
marriage was going to be a quiet affair in many ways, a
quiet life together, for the most part a simple existence.
She was going to be in her element, looking after him
and loving him, content, fulfilled, just to do that. And
equally, in other respects it wasn't going to be peaceful.
Adam would always say bluntly what he was thinking,
he would lay down the law, and she would always
resist, with her innate independence and with sheer
deliberate, impishness. That was her basic nature.

He brought the drinks over, muttering something else
disparaging about the living-room. 'Wait till you see
your new home in Tuscany. Now there's——' He
stopped, looking at her. 'If you don't say you'll marry

me, and say it quickly, I'll——'

'I'll marry you,' she said, quickly. She didn't want to hear any threats from him, he would only carry them out! Laughing, she took the glass from him. 'Here's to us, my darling Adam. And to my new home in Italy. Of course, you appreciate I might want to refurnish and redecorate when I see it . . .'

Adam raised an eyebrow, grinned, raised his glass to her, took a swallow and put it down on the stainless steel and glass coffee table. 'You're going to find it very different from this place.'

'I'm glad to hear it.'

'And it's nothing like Dolly's house!'

'No place on earth could be like Dolly's house!'

'Speaking of which—Mum, I mean—why don't we phone her, tell her our news?'

'Because she's gone away for a few weeks.' She laughed again at the look on his face. 'Didn't you know?'

'Gone *away*? What does that mean? I have tried ringing her, several times, but I assumed she was out. Let's face it, she's hardly ever in!'

Kate was giggling. Good old Aunt Dolly! She'd even neglected to tell Adam! 'She's gone away with some people from the bridge club. She'll be back on Monday, as far as I can gather from Mum. My mum's had several postcards from her. I've only had one. And we can't phone her at all, the card was postmarked in Scotland but she didn't mention where she was staying!'

Adam was laughing. 'Isn't she the greatest?'

'The greatest!' Kate snuggled up to him. It had been too long since she'd touched him. She put a hand on his face, smiling up into his eyes. 'We could ring my parents, let them know. Or shall I make you something to eat before we start ringing people? I know you're hungry——'

'Later,' he said, taking the glass from her hands.
'Come here, Kate. Closer, darling, closer...' He
brought his mouth down to hers. 'We'll make our
phone calls later, we'll eat later.' He was speaking
against her lips now, brushing her mouth with his.
'There's something better we could be doing right now.
As you know full well, my darling Kate, I'm hungry in
more ways than one...'

Harlequin Presents

Coming Next Month

951 SURRENDER, MY HEART Lindsay Armstrong
The man who has shown an Australian widow nothing but contempt suddenly takes her to an island resort at Surfers Paradise—the perfect getaway for lovers, not enemies!

952 CAPTIVES OF THE PAST Robyn Donald
To prevent her ex-husband from marrying her stepsister and hurting her, too, a New Zealander returns home and again faces the misguided judgment of the only man she's ever loved.

953 HIDDEN TREASURES Emma Goldrick
Protection from her money-hungry relatives is what this Cape Cod heiress needs, and a hard-to-read lawyer offers it—in the form of marriage. But with forty million dollars at stake, who can she trust?

954 MAID TO MEASURE Roberta Leigh
Disguising herself as a maid to put off the proposal of a French aristocratic suitor seems like a good idea until it becomes clear he's against the match, too—and intends to marry in haste to avoid it.

955 HAWK'S PREY Carole Mortimer
An English journalist's latest scoop involves her boss, the man who used to be her guardian. Why can't he just confide in her—man to woman—instead of treating her like a child and pulling her off the story?

956 BITTER LEGACY Sandra K. Rhoades
When her stepfather insists she marry, a Vancouver heiress flees to the wilderness only to become stranded with a take-charge businessman who seems to know all about her. It could be a setup.

957 YESTERDAY'S MIRROR Sophie Weston
Although she's used to her father's tirades, a disillusioned daughter is appalled when he orders her—within earshot of everyone—to entertain an English lord and seduce him into selling his publishing interests.

958 THE DARKER SIDE OF LOVING Yvonne Whittal
A widow's matchmaking uncle introduces her to a dynamic hotel owner who senses her reluctance to love again. But his parting words—"We'll meet again"—sound more like a threat than a promise.

Six exciting series for you every month... from Harlequin

Harlequin Romance·
The series that started it all

Tender, captivating and heartwarming...
love stories that sweep you off to faraway places
and delight you with the magic of love.

◆

Harlequin Presents·

Powerful contemporary love stories...as individual as the women who read them

The No. 1 romance series...
exciting love stories for you, the woman of today...
a rare blend of passion and dramatic realism.

◆

Harlequin Superromance®
It's more than romance...
it's Harlequin Superromance

A sophisticated, contemporary romance-fiction
series, providing you with a longer,
more involving read...a richer mix of complex plots,
realism and adventure.